EXPLAIN!

- A themed anthology -

**Presented by
Creative Writing Institute**

ISBN: 978-1-927296-13-4

Dedication

by Deborah Owen, CEO

As far back as I can remember, my mother said she wanted me to be a writer. That thought drove me to place third in my first writing contest at age 13. I sold a number of articles, including approximately 40 items that I researched, drafted and sold to the American Legion for their 75th Anniversary edition. Mom told me she was very proud. My husband and children also gave me the support I needed, but not every writer is that fortunate.

Who believes in you? A parent, sibling, aunt or uncle? A teacher, neighbor, friend? Those of us who have such support are the luckiest writers on earth, but you may be standing alone. If so, there are some things you can do to help yourself.

1. Join a local writer's group. It is the level playing field where you will find others like yourself.

2. Join an online writer's group. You will definitely find friends there.

3. Confide in your friends. Tell them you would like to become a selling writer. Give them the opportunity to show support.

4. But if you have no one at all, go look in the mirror and say out loud, "I AM a writer, and no one is going to talk me out of it. I will learn the tools of my trade so I can succeed."

Remember, selling your work is *not* what makes you a writer. *Writing* is what makes you a writer. A hobby writer is no less a writer than one who sells his/her work. As in all trades, there are varying degrees of achievement, but there is only one place to begin... and that is at the bottom.

Creative Writing Institute's 2016 anthology is dedicated to my mother, and wanting to please her drove me to writing, but this edition is also dedicated to every person who offers support to a writer as well as the writers who cheer themselves on to victory.

Just keep writing!

http://www.CreativeWritingInstitute.com/

CONTENTS

Acknowledgements
by Deborah Owen, CEO

Welcome to Creative Writing Institute's fourth annual anthology!

This collection contains three short story winners, three honorable mentions (a three-way tie!), judges' picks, (stories that did not place but were recommended for publication), the contest judges, invited guests, best-selling authors and CWI staff who will all add a little spice to the mix.

We would also like to thank Southern Star Publications and editor, Jay Hirst, for making this book a reality. Creative Writing Institute also extends its gratitude to Nicky Hirst, who proofread the entire book, and last, but by no means least, our heartfelt thanks to Jianna Higgins, who coordinated the contest, assisted with the book cover, edited and proofread… and pulled her hair out in the process.

And then there are the short story contest judges who sacrificially labored together to select these stories. There would be no contest without them! Thank you:

Head judge: Jo Popek
Coordinating judge: Jianna Higgins
Judge: L. Edward Carroll
Judge: Emily-Jane Hills Orford
Judge: Diane M. Robinson

Thank you so much, Caleb Pirtle III, for writing our Foreword. And that brings us to those who have so kindly allowed us to publish their work in our 2016 anthology. We wish you the very best as you march forth into the unknown.

Last, but not least, we thank you, the reader, for supporting these authors and Creative Writing Institute by ordering your copy of our 2016 anthology. Without you, all efforts would be in vain. And now Creative Writing Institute proudly presents its fourth anthology EXPLAIN!

Foreword

by Caleb Pirtle III

It's always the same. We writers hardly ever change. We mostly write about strangers. We haven't met them. We don't know they exist until they walk onto one of our pages. They usually show up when we least expect them. We certainly didn't know they were on the way.

A stranger comes to town with a gun. A stranger dies. A stranger buries him. The stranger has a secret? The stranger disappears. Which one? Doesn't matter. They're all strangers anyway.

And we only have one question for them.

Can you explain how that happened?

A stranger finds a woman. Sometimes the stranger is a woman. Two strangers meet. Two strangers fall in love. By now, they aren't strangers anymore. They are family. And, generally, if we write their stories well and accurately, they are a dysfunctional family.

One by one, page after page, their lives become ever clearer.

They tell us what happened.

They explain how it happened.

We are often shocked. We are often stunned. We had no idea.

Some strangers search for the spotlight. Some strangers remain in the shadows. The quiet strangers, the strangers with nothing to say, are the strangers who intrigue us and captivate our imaginations. As John Wayne always said: "When a scene in a motion picture has three characters, the one who doesn't say anything is the most interesting person in the room."

Who is he? What is he thinking? Is he important? Is he dangerous? What is he hiding? Why doesn't he say something? Can he solve the mystery? Or is *he* the mystery?

Don't know. He's a stranger to me.

We know what happened.

We're now waiting for him to explain how it happened.

In great stories, we know his name. We know her name. We know what each looks like. We know how they dress. We even know their backstories. But do we really know them? Those are the ones we remember long after the story ends.

It happened. They explained how it happened, and sometimes it is very difficult to explain. What choices did they have? What choices did they make? Which road did they take? Should they have gone the other way? We know, and they know, life will never be quite the same again.

They were nothing more than strangers who chanced to come into our lives, but we do love our strangers.

I recently read a quote that makes a lot of sense. I don't remember who said it. I don't recall where I read it, but the quote is definitely worth remembering.

I like beginnings because they're so full of promise.

The first page of a book. The first day of a job. The first date. The first kiss. The first time you fall in love. The first time you face a crisis. The first time you face life on its own terms. The first time life knocks you to your knees. The first time you stand back up. The first kick of a good liqueur. The first time you hold your baby. The first time you cry. The first time someone comes along to wipe the tears away.

I like beginnings because I know there's always more to come.

The more I think about it, the more I realize that life is much like a novel. We don't read it. We live it. Each day is a blank page. Each day is a new beginning. Each day has a moment of conflict. We laugh. We cry. We fall in love. We fall out of love. We are disappointed. We know how hard life can be. We know how difficult it is to find a measure of peace. It can be as difficult as finding the next word to put on an empty page.

Each day holds at least one crisis. We can win. We can lose. We can start over.

That's the reason we have new chapters in our lives. We can't quit.

As long as we have a breath to draw, we have another page to live or to write. Some chapters are longer than others. Some chapters are better than others. We fill those pages with the characters who come along to touch our lives. Some we like. Some we don't. Some we fear. Most are strangers. A few we've known forever. But we need them all. What would life be… what would our story be without them?

There is, however, one major difference between life and a novel. In our story, we know how it ends. We write the final punch line. We tie up the loose ends. We know who does and who doesn't live happily ever after.

But life ends before we realize it. Life ends long before we're ready. Someone else will have to write the final paragraph. It's always the writer who has the final word. It's always the writer who can explain what went right, what went wrong, how our story happened, and why our story happened. Who will read our stories? I'm betting on strangers. They deserve an explanation.

***

BIO: Caleb Pirtle III is the author of more than seventy books, including the Ambrose Lincoln series: *Secrets of the Dead*, *Conspiracy of Lies*, and *Night Side of Dark*. He writes both noir thrillers and historical fiction with a dark edge. He prefers living in the past when times were hard and usually desperate.

His nonfiction book, *XIT: The American Cowboy* became one of the best-selling art books of all time.

Pirtle is a graduate of The University of Texas in Austin and became the first student at the university to win the National William Randolph Hearst Award for feature writing. Several of his books and articles have received national and regional awards.

Pirtle has written three teleplays: *Gambler V: Playing for Keeps*, a mini-series for CBS starring Kenny Rogers, Loni Anderson, Dixie Carter, and Mariska Hargitay, *Wildcat: The Story of Sarah Delaney and the Doodlebug Man*, a CBS TV movie, and *The Texas Rangers,* a TV movie for John Milius and TNT television. He wrote two novels for Berkeley based on the Gambler series: *Dead Man's Hand* and *Jokers Are Wild.*

Pirtle was a newspaper reporter for the *Fort Worth Star-Telegram* and served ten years as travel editor for *Southern Living Magazine*. He was editorial director for a Dallas custom publisher for more than 25 years.

The Pond at Summer's End
by Martha Readyoff
First Place Winner 2016 Contest

The cool flow ran over her hands… a quiet ecstasy on that hot day. She stood there, staring into the exhausting greenness of mid-August, leaning against the kitchen counter, lazing in the soothing sensation that flowed and bubbled through her fingers.

She drifted through this time as she had in the dreamtime of her childhood, lilting upon the slow-moving stream of whim and desire. Half-reluctantly, she shook her hands over the sink and allowed pink drops to plink the unwashed teacups that chided her ever so softly.

A Siamese cat curled in and out of her bare legs. His tail followed behind, tickling the backs of her knees. "Hello there, William Morris." Her words drifted down to the floor. "What shall we two do this afternoon?"

She leaned over and picked up the little cat that went limp in her arms. "Gumbie Cat," she said as she laid him over her shoulder like a living fur stole.

He hung there, content and purring.

"Oh my, you're too hot," she said, and placed him gently on the floor.

He flicked his tail and walked away to sulk.

"Don't be like that, William Wordsworth." But she had already turned on the faucet, relished the soft, cool flow and waited for it to get chilly and icy. She scooped it in cupped hands and splashed her face a couple of times until cool rills trickled down her neck and shoulders.

She rinsed a leftover glass from breakfast and filled it, gulped it down and filled it again. She took it to the porch, noting the whine and bang of the old screen door. It was as much a part of the summer chorus as cicadas and birds. It bore the sound of freedom.

Only a week before school started again. The end of summer. Her little students were no longer allowed a childhood, and she tired of the fluttering parents that dithered her. No time for comfort. No time for books or writing or even thinking.

Ignore those thoughts. You're a piece of flotsam on a slow summer stream.

It was like practicing forgetting. Vaguely, she wondered if trying to forget would, in old age, make one addled. It seemed like a good hypothesis for a scientist to study, but like other thoughts, her mind slid off to something else.

The over-bright day seemed to her a dream, the way the edges of things were misty and blurred, which was fine with her. She snatched her straw hat with the faded paper roses from its hook and walked onto the thick green lawn. Absently, she wriggled her toes in the grass, finished her drink and put the glass on the bottom porch step. The cat mewed pleadingly from the kitchen window. "Okay, William Carlos Williams," and she lifted the cat onto her shoulder where he perched parrot-like.

She stepped without destination across the lawn. The filmy white sundress floated above her ankles as she passed into the small grove of peach trees where perfumed air mingled with ripe fruit. She plucked one big peach, so velvet soft and warm in her hand. She held it up and inhaled the aroma, filling her lungs, smiling and blinking dreamily. Her mouth watered instantly, but she looked at it a moment longer, eating its furry pink skin with her eyes, always insatiable for beauty. It tasted as pink and perfect as it looked. She devoured it and wiped the sticky juice from her chin with the back of her hand. The cat reached over and licked the messy swipe from her cheek, then leapt off her shoulder and ran to the end of the grove.

The unicorn stood as it always did at the end of the grove, its white coat grey-streaked with years of weather. She patted its shoulder and ran her fingers down the marble face. She laid her face against its cool neck. "Salvation," she whispered, and the unicorn snorted and flicked its pretty head. "Hush now. One day we will run away. You will carry me across the world to a place where emails don't exist. Where no one has goals or plans. Where no one is ignored or neglected by those they love." She gazed into its stony eye.

At the head of the trail, wandering into the woods, William sat licking his paw and rubbing his ears.

"Wait for me, William B. Yeats!" she called.

William looked up and trotted playfully down the path into the woods.

"Wait! William! Wait!" she called again and flitted after him. The way her toes grazed the grass made her giddy, as though she could fly down the hill toward the woods.

The path was wide and grassy, narrowing and growing rocky the farther in she went. The woods were close and dim but cooler, the air a watery green with faint rippling leaf shadows. She slowed to a saunter, looking for the cat.

In the rhododendron bushes to the left crouched the faun, forever playing upon his pipes.

"Hello, sir," she said as she sat on the grass cross-legged before him. "Have you seen my kitty?"

The faun replied with a fixed gaze.

She closed her eyes and let his music fill her ears. It was pure music, as sweet as summer peaches, as sad as autumn, with no commercial interruptions. When she opened her eyes again, he was standing, ready to lead her away. He winked before sitting in the stillness again.

"Another day, then?" she nodded to him, rose and continued down the path. A *meow* sounded, just ahead and around the bend in the trail, where an old cherry tree struggled to free itself from brambles and underbrush.

"Coming, my William!"

She made her way along the rocky path, resting in the little gazebo. A garden of fairy houses sprang up here and there like mushrooms, but she sat on the bench swing, leaning back, crossing her ankles. A heaviness gathered in her chest as spots marred the floor and before she could remember to forget, she was crying. The tears came without fanfare at first, as though her eyes leaked a well-spring of salt water that made her body quiver with sobs.

It was the world's fault, with all its buying and selling and meetings and processing of everything and everyone, but the real problem was her *in* the world.

"Education is the indoctrin . . ." she muttered between sniffles.

"Shhh…" said the fairies that hovered at her ears. "Hush… hush… all will be well…" they whirred.

"All will be well… all will be well," she echoed in a falsetto tone.

They glimmered all about, black and gold, their

queen slightly larger, dressed in emerald and cochineal.

"Will it?" she begged the queen. "Will it really all be well?"

The queen hovered before her eyes and brushed the tears on her cheeks with a whisk of feathery wings. The queen had a tiny face, decorated with a delicate nose and quick black eyes. "It will be well when you find your cat."

The fairies hummed and buzzed behind her as she traveled the path that descended even more steeply. The cool fragrance of the garden was lost to an odor, damp and sweet, like a deep well.

"William!" she quoted her favorite poet. "You are old, father William, the young man said!"

The steep trail opened to a pond. Still and dark and cool, lined by redolent pines and sylphic birches. A great willow grew from a small island in the middle, its mournful branches skimming the water. Under the tree, William lay at peace, looking across the pond. His blue eyes danced like bright distant stars.

She cocked her head. "Explain how that happened," she whispered to the fairies. "How did he get over there?"

"William! William Faulkner! My William!" she called. Her voice cracked.

She stepped into the water. Her white dress floated all around her, ghostly. She began to swim. "William!" she called as she swam with frog-like grace toward the island and the little cat. "William…"

Far beneath the surface emerged the faces of mermaids.

She saw their scales, emeralds glittering in the dark water, their long hair like seaweed curling around lithe fish-bodies. Pale limbs, luminous, beckoned.

"Come!" their voices carried in silver bubbles that popped on the air.

And she stopped swimming toward the island where the cat lay watching with starry eyes.

"Come!" the mermaids bubbled.

She looked once more at the cat. "I love you," she said.

He blink-kissed her, in his cat kind of way.

Then she looked down at the peaceful gloom beneath, reached for a mermaid's hand, and smiled as the fish-girl pulled her down, down, ever down into the kingdom of the broken-hearted and the wistful dreamers.

He came home that evening, put his briefcase in its spot by the door and loosened his tie. "I'm home," he said. Tired, he did not wonder why there was no reply, nor did he worry until he saw the dried blood on the knife, the spattered sink and the red footsteps to the back porch. He called her name as he followed the trail, found the broken wine glass and the empty bottle of absinthe on the step. He called again as he followed red traces of her, dark in the dusk light, through the old dead peach grove and down the path to the pond. He cried her name, pulled her from the water and she lay dripping in his arms as he raised his wail to the moon's Cheshire crescent grin.

***

The Given
by Jennifer A. Doss
Second Place Winner 2016 Contest

Mariah refused to look back. Her parents, sister and most of the village walked her to the edge of the mountain. Tears flowed down many of their faces and Mariah felt a twinge of regret for not saying goodbye to everyone. She was only 11. Her parents could've waited a few more months. After all, she got around fine, even with her club foot. She pulled her weight in the village, doing chores without complaint, but village laws were absolute. A child born with a deformity could stay until they turned 11. If by then, the deformity hadn't healed itself, or was severe enough to affect their well-being, they were 'given.' Those who were 'given' were snatched and never seen again.

Mariah remembered how sick at heart she was after Miss Catherine's baby, Josh, had been 'given' due to a cleft palate that kept him from closing his mouth, even to nurse.

For six months, Miss Catherine dribbled milk into his mouth before the elders ordered he be 'given.' She cried for weeks and still rarely left home.

Mariah had tried to comfort her with special herb tea, but she just stared past her and mindlessly patted Mariah's arm. Now it was her turn, and she wouldn't give them the satisfaction of seeing her cry.

The procession stopped when they reached the first stony outcropping. Only the 'given' could go further. If the villagers trod too close, the red thing might also take them.

Sammie, Mariah's best friend, gripped her hand as they walked together. They had said their goodbyes the night before so Mariah jerked away when they reached the rocks.

Her heart slammed inside her chest and tears brimmed against her lashes. Barely able to put one foot in front of the other, the girl limped along. Fifty steps before she was swept away forever. How many times had she counted the steps as nature's other *mistakes* walked this path? She willed her feet forward... 36... 37... she could feel their eyes burn against her back... 43... 44... she stumbled on the rocks. Stupid foot! She couldn't even die in perfection.

"Mariah!" Someone cut Sammie's scream short and dragged her away.

Mariah paused, but did not turn around. Her heart broke for Sammie who would have to deal with the loss of her friend.

She forced her right foot forward, beginning her march again, fighting for every breath as she entered the cage. Suddenly, she was no longer on the ground. Trees streaked past in a blur. Liquid dampened her clothes. Straining, she turned her head to see the thing. Red scaly wings. A blur of red legs sprinting across the ground.

Mariah screamed and shook the bars but the thing gave a guttural growl. The door opened when she fell against it and she tumbled out. The creature's eyes grew large as she crawled. It opened its mighty jaws and roared. Jagged teeth pierced her flesh like dozens of needles. Another scream left her throat, and everything faded to black.

An hour later, her eyes fluttered in the dark. Where was she? Home? She tried to move and groaned with the effort. Pain shot through her limbs, and she winced when she touched the shallow wounds. The creature! Where was it? How was she still alive?

Whatever was beneath her was soft and squishy. As her eyes adjusted to the darkness, she could make out a stick cage that encircled her. She seemed to be lying on soft red fur. No. She definitely was not home. Heaving herself to a standing position, she peeked through the sticks. The wood intertwined and rose on each side. She appeared to be in a cave. A shudder ran through her. Was it waiting for her to try to escape? She sighed and tilted her head back. The top of her cage was open – and then reality dawned on her. It wasn't a cage. It was a nest! All she had to do was climb out.

From somewhere in the cave she heard a scuffling and then a thud. Mariah held her breath, frozen in place. The creature must have heard her. No… it sounded like… crying. Like a young child.

"Uh, hello?" she said softly.

"Wwwhhhooo, who's there?" A small, shaky voice replied.

"I'm Mariah. Who are you?"

"I'm Devin. Are you a creature?"

Mariah chuckled. "I'm a girl. A red creature brought me here."

"The red one? The big blue meanie brought me," Devin said. "Mariah, I'm so scared."

"Me, too. Keep your voice down. Can you see any creatures in here?"

"No. Blue meanie flied away and – I don't know where I am."

Mariah's eyes filled with fresh tears, and she swallowed hard to force the lump in her throat down."

"I think I can get to you. Hold on. As soon as I

climb out of this nest, I'll find you. Okay?"

"Okay."

Her right foot propelled her upward as she wedged her club foot between branches for balance. It took more effort and time than expected, and Devin called several times to make sure she was still coming. Finally, she crested the top of the nest and stopped to catch her breath, taking stock of her surroundings. Moonlight dimly lit the cave revealing more nests.

"Devin, where are you?" she said, barely above a whisper.

"Over here."

She turned toward the voice. "I'm at the top of the nest. As soon as I climb down, I'll find you."

But going down was more difficult than anticipated. And if she fell, there was no soft fur on the ground.

"Devin? Keep talking so I can find you."

"I don't know what to say, but I'm over here."

Mariah limped from nest to nest until she found the right one, and there, peeping through the branches, was a boy about four years old.

"Well, hi there," she said, peeping back at him.

Straw-colored hair drooped over blue eyes. "Hi. Can you get me out?" he said.

"Climb like I did. I'll be right here the whole time."

"I tried, but I fell down. My hands don't work right," he said, looking at gnarled hands that bore stumpy fingers.

"I have a bad foot," she said. "You can do it, Devin. Try real hard."

"I want my mommy," he said, melting into sobs.

"Shh... keep your voice down. Pretend I'm your mommy and you're going to climb out of that nasty old nest and into my arms. Try, Devin. Please try before the blue meanie comes back."

Reluctantly, Devin started to climb. His strong legs propelled him upward, but his hand slipped. With much cajoling, he finally made it over the top and slowly began to climb down. "My hands hurt," he said with a whine. "I can't make it."

"Yes, you can. Remember, I'm your mommy and I have my arms out to…"

"Mariah, help! I can't hold…"

And before Mariah could answer, the small form floated through the air, crying all the way down. Mariah lurched forward and spread her arms wide. Devin fell onto her and they rolled together. "Are you okay?" she said.

"My hands hurt, but I'm okay. Mariah, you catched me! Thank you!" He threw his tiny arms around her neck.

"You were a brave boy."

They cowered behind a large rock. "Don't let the blue meanie get me."

"How *did* the big blue meanie catch you? Explain how that happened."

Devin hung his head. "I couldn't do nothin' right cuz of my hands. They said I was made wrong and I had to go away. Mommy cried, and I cried. The big blue meanie flied with me and hurt me with his claws and he brought me here. Nobody but Mommy wanted me anyway."

"I know what you mean," Mariah said, wrapping her arms around him. "They called me a *mistake*. My foot made it hard to keep up with everyone, so they sent me away, too."

They heard a loud fluttering as red, blue and yellow creatures descended into the cave. Now that

Mariah could see them clearly, they looked like furry dragons covered with round dog-like faces.

"Cree, cree, cree cree." The red one cocked its head.

The yellow one screamed back, "Craw, craw, craw!" In its huge talons was a piece of blue fabric that fluttered down.

Curious, Mariah reached for it when the creatures looked away. It was a blue shirt, about Devin's size. And there was blood streaked across it. Devin's eyes bugged and he opened his mouth to scream, but Mariah clamped her hand over his face. "Shh," she whispered in his ear. "We have to find a way out before we end up like the person who wore this."

He nodded through tears, his eyes as wide as saucers.

"Croot, croot, croot, croot," the big blue one said.

The yellow one responded by scratching the ground, flinging dirt everywhere.

"Follow me, and don't make a sound." Mariah crept around, keeping large rocks between them and the creatures still engaged in conversation, but the screeching stopped abruptly. Mariah stopped, staring in unbelief. The blue and red creatures folded their wings around the yellow one as though comforting it.

Devin hadn't noticed that she stopped and careened into her, knocking both to the ground and drawing the attention of all three creatures.

"Run!" Mariah shouted. "If you find a way out, yell," but Devin stood frozen in place as the blue one reached for him.

"No!" Mariah said as she dove between them, shoving Devin out of the way. "Run. Get out. Hide!"

The blue monster pecked at Mariah. She tried to roll away, but claws lifted and wrapped about her.

"Mariah!"

"Run, Devin. Run."

Devin took off at full speed, circling the cave, searching for an exit.

"There's no way out!" he screamed at her.

"Keep looking," Mariah said. The thing dropped her into the red creature's nest.

"Oomph... don't look back, Devin. Just find a way out." Mariah heard a scream, followed by a whoosh as the blue monster winged by and dropped Devin into the nest beside her.

"Cree? Cree?" the yellow one said, tilting its head back and forth.

"Croot."

"Craw! Craw, craw."

Like arrows loosed from a bow, the creatures descended on them and then shot up and through the hole in the cave, both children tightly bound in their claws.

Despair enveloped Mariah as Devin begged her to save them. She had failed to rescue him and now this thing would have a good dinner. Her thoughts moved to the child who wore the bloody blue shirt and pent up tears streaked down her dirty cheeks.

The creatures flew over the treetops and into the clouds for what seemed like hours. As the sun crested, they landed in an open field and deposited the children on the ground.

Something rustled in the nearby trees. Something was coming for them.

Mariah grabbed Devin and held him tight.

The underbrush swished, and out stepped... a girl about her Mariah's age with long, silky black hair.

Skin covered the place where her right eye should have been.

Mariah shouted a warning. "Run! Run! These creatures will eat you!"

But the girl laughed and kept walking toward them.

Other people parted the tall weeds and stepped into the open. A silver-haired man with one arm and a woman with one leg, followed by a wave of children. Some were led. Some used walking sticks. Some were carried. They kept coming, one after another.

A grinning toddler. Something about the child seemed familiar. It was his mouth. It had a gaping hole in it. He was Miss Catherine's baby!

And all at once Mariah understood. Each person had a disability. Like her. Like Devin.

"Welcome," a man said. "This is your new home. We call it Haven."

So many people introduced themselves that Mariah would never remember all their names. She scooped up Josh, wishing Miss Catherine could see her little boy.

Mariah turned to the old gent. "I don't understand. I thought…"

The yellow creature made a sound and Mariah turned to stare. It perched flat on the ground as though it were sitting on eggs. The children shouted with glee and climbed atop the creature's back and she knew this was a place created just for them.

For the first time, she knew she truly belonged.

***

Prime Timers
by Karen Rush
Third Place Winner 2016 Contest

Jennifer was drawn to old people. She liked how they smelled of dusting powder, and cottage cheese mingled with pineapple. Occasionally, there was the slight prickly scent of mothballs, but she overlooked that because their oversized cardigans were so endearing, especially if a button was missing. And the fuzzy, green tennis balls taped to the front of their walkers? Adorable.

Their bifocal glasses touched her soul, and because she cared so much for the aged, she knew she was the perfect person to lead the activities at Prime Time Palace. But after three months, Winifred Winston, the director, was not so sure. The residents remained, for the most part, uninspired.

"Tell me again, about today's activity or inactivity, as the case may be." Winifred peered at Jennifer over her glasses, her lips pursed.

"Oh, yes ma'am. Today's activity will entail a lot of brain work including following directions, employing the imagination, making decisions in a time crunch, all the while incorporating physical movement."

"Hmmm…and that's happening, how?"

"We're going to Kroger."

Five activity directors had come and gone in the past three years with the same standard regimen of activities dotting the calendar. From pre-school crayoned valentines to Easter baskets stuffed with cheap chocolate and breath mints. Church choirs came to sing Christmas carols while an overfed Santa with a fake beard and dirty gloves handed out primly wrapped gifts of cotton handkerchiefs and warm socks. Some days, there was a bingo game in the dining hall, the numbers called out by one of the *younger* old men in a worn, ill-fitting tux.

Other days, a woman with a bad hair style, dyed jet black, played the piano as she sang old show tunes in a voice too high to be pleasant. Once, a group of local square dancers with colorful flouncy dresses showed up with men in matching shirts, but they never came back after Carol swatted at their ankles with her cane as they do-si-doed past her.

The Prime Timers were bored with it all and endured these activities with stifled yawns. They could accept being old, it was the tedium they couldn't abide.

By the time Jennifer appeared, the residents were wary and worn. She was definitely peppy and happy and full of new ideas, but they found themselves too tired to care. They shunned the challenges she offered to their complacency.

Then Priscilla saw the tiny butterfly tattooed just below Jennifer's collarbone. That was interesting, but could she be trusted if she did that to her body? No, they were safe right there slumped on the couch in front of *Family Feud*. Wasn't it about time to die anyway?

When Jennifer announced the Mystery Ramble, only four residents raised their hands to sign up. Her youthful exuberance unsettled them and when Carol noticed Sam still had his hands in his pockets, she quickly lowered hers, claiming she wasn't really signing up, but was stretching instead.

Sam shrugged, and then raised his hand. There

were only two men living at Prime Time Palace…
Sam and another man who rarely left his room. Sam
was the one all the women clamored for, even though
he was a bit grouchy.

It took thirty minutes for them to gather and load
into the van as it idled by the front door. "Prime Time
Palace" was written in elegant green script on both
sides. Tiny pieces of glitter were embedded in the
paint and they sparkled in the sun.

Sam slapped at the words as he boarded the van.
"This place looks like it's a fun, exciting place to
live," he said to Jennifer, as she stood by the step.
"But guess what? It's not."

"Maybe today will be different? Let's go with a
good attitude," Jennifer said.

Sam snorted.

Lenora was already seated by the window, her
purse clutched in her lap. "It's going to be fine," she
muttered softly to herself.

Sam sat down next to her. "Sure it's going to be
fine. You know what this big Mystery Ramble is? It's
a trip to the grocery store for Pete's sake. What could
possibly go wrong?"

"Do I need money?" Lenora opened her purse
and dumped it onto her lap. Her skirt caught the
meager contents: crumpled tissues, a small black
comb, and a roll of lifesavers. "Here we go," she said,
as she held up the lifesavers. "It's going to be fine."

"Yeah, it'll be fine." Sam yawned as he threw
his arm over the back of the seat.

Carol stumbled into the van, jabbing her cane
into the floorboard. A black beauty mark was penciled
above her lip and large dangling earrings pulled at her
lobes. Her hair was tinted a vague orange and her
scalp showed through.

"Is that a sword?" Lenora asked.

"A sword? What on earth would I be doing with a sword, huh Lenora, would you tell me that? You are really getting looney-toons. Everybody knows it." Carol plopped down on the seat in front of them.

"Oh." Lenora lowered her eyes. She fidgeted with the clasp on her purse.

"Aw, don't you worry about her. You'll always be a sweetheart, Lenora, and she's nothing more than a loudmouth floozy."

"I heard that, Sam."

"Well turn down your hearing aid if you don't want to hear what people say about you," he said to a scowling Carol.

Lenora rocked gently back and forth. "It's going to be fine. It's going to be fine."

Priscilla was last on and took the seat next to Carol, her walker clumsily knocking at Carol's knees.

Carol sighed, and then shifted in her seat to stare out the window. A small blip of gas fouled the air.

"And we're off, adventurers!" Jennifer said, as she pulled into traffic. She began to sing, "C'est Si Bon," but none of the passengers joined in, and some had nodded off before the van crossed the boulevard.

The director, Winifred Winston, was waiting for them when they returned to Prime Time Palace. She watched with a cool eye as they entered the lobby.

Sam led the way but stopped as Mrs. Winston held one finger poised mid-air.

They gathered around her and turned as Jennifer came in.

She was dabbing at something on the front of her shirt and faltered when she saw the director. She offered a weak smile.

"Jennifer. I've just gotten off the phone with the

manager at Kroger. She was quite upset. It seems Prime Time Palace is no longer welcome. Can you believe it? No longer welcome? It's a grocery store. Who gets banned from a grocery store?"

The Prime Timers glanced at each other. Sam crossed his arms over his chest and whispered something that made them all giggle.

Jennifer looked at them wondering how they could possibly be the same placid people who had boarded the van just hours before.

Priscilla's shoes were wet, Carol had lost an earring, and someone smelled distinctly of blue cheese.

"Banned?" Jennifer said. "Banned?"

Winifred Winston nodded. "Explain how that happened."

"Well. I'm not sure really…"

"It was the Mystery Ramble," Sam said. "Face it, Jennifer, it was a crazy idea."

"And that ridiculous, 'put on your thinking berets and pretend to be in France'?" added Carol.

"You had us close our eyes. 'Think France, breathe France, be one with France'," Priscilla said, as she waved her arms. She looked directly at Jennifer. "That was stupid."

"And then we had to search the store for French souvenirs?"

Jennifer felt a small lump forming in her throat. It had seemed like such a good idea, fun and different, and now she did her best not to cry.

"But I did find French fries and quiche Lorraine," Priscilla said. "And Lenora here has French onion soup mix."

"Oh. Is that what this is?" Lenora shook the box. "I liked France. It was very cold, and bright. I heard there was a clean-up on aisle ten. Was that by the Eiffel Tower?"

"Nope, it was around the corner from the Arc de Triomphe," Sam said, grinning.

"Oh, that's right," said Lenora. "Sometimes I get a little confused." She put the soup mix in her purse.

"That sounds innocent enough," said Winifred Winston. "What did you find, Sam?"

"Aw, I didn't find much. I wasn't really into it," Sam said, rolling back on his heels, his hands in his pockets.

Carol nudged him. "Go on," she whispered.

"Nah, it was nothing."

"It was everything."

"Yeah? Well, okay. I picked up a bottle or two of champagne," Sam said.

"And?"

"And I went behind the marked down bakery rack. It's over by the health food. No one ever goes down that aisle so it's pretty deserted."

"And?"

"And I popped the cork. So what? I'm a bad boy, shoot me."

Winifred Winston took a deep breath. Her gaze fell on each of the Prime Timers. "Did anyone else partake of stolen goods?"

Priscilla raised her hand. "I didn't mean to. I was looking through the cheese case when I saw him back there with the champagne." She squelched a small burp as she leaned on her walker. "Turns out, I'm kind of a party girl."

"I was coming from the bakery with a hard, fresh baguette. I'm always looking for a good baguette," Carol said, as she winked at Sam. "And I heard this psst, psst and there was Sam offering me a swig, too."

"Oh good Heavens," Winifred Winston said, fanning herself. "And was there something about a food fight?"

"Oh, that." Priscilla looked around. "It wasn't really a fight…"

"You were throwing brussel sprouts at people," Carol said.

Priscilla shrugged. "I thought Brussels was in France."

"I threw cabbage," Lenora said. "I did. That was me. I think."

"It was you alright, looney-toons. But I was the one who yelled, 'off with their heads!' as the cabbage rolled around. I was one with France. I'm very avant-garde when I drink," Carol said.

"And then you," Priscilla pointed at Sam, "starting singing 'I see London, I see France, I see…'"

"Yeah, well, with all that lifting and throwing I caught a glimpse of Lenora here. Those underpants were not what I was expecting."

Lenora blushed. Now Sam knew. Some days, she forgot to wear her panties.

Winifred Winston clapped her hands. "People, people, is there anything else? Jennifer?"

"Oh, Mrs. Winston," Jennifer said. "I'm just as surprised by all this as you are. I didn't realize this was going on. We were supposed to rendezvous in the bakery. We were going to have croissants and café au lait."

"But there was that big crash," Priscilla said.

"I think it was the Metro," Lenora said, as she tugged at Priscilla's sleeve. "Weren't we running for the Metro?"

"No, it wasn't the Metro. It was the pastry

display."

"Did we catch it?"

"I think we're catching it now," Sam said. "Look, Winifred, I don't think it would have been so bad except that Marie Antoinette here," he nodded towards Carol, "yelled, 'Let them eat cake!' just as the manager showed up."

"That manager knows nothing of Joie de vivre," Carol said. "Then this one," she put her arm around Priscilla's shoulder, "suddenly had a puddle at her feet. Eau de toilette."

"It was the champagne. I have a small bladder."

Lenora began to whisper, "It's going to be fine, it's going to be fine," as she dug through her purse.

"Lenora, please stop your rambling. It is not going to be fine," the director said. "Jennifer, I'm holding you completely responsible. There will be consequences. Mystery Ramble… the very idea."

The Prime Timers looked from Winifred Winston to Jennifer.

"Yes, she was completely responsible," Priscilla said.

"Mystery Ramble, the very great idea," Carol said.

"Most fun I've had since my keys were taken away," Sam said.

"Voila." Lenora handed Jennifer the lifesavers, then she turned to Winifred Winston. "Fait accompli," she said, as she snapped her purse shut.

***

Boomerang!
by Ronnie Dauber
Honorable Mention Winner 2016 Contest

The boys hid in the bushes and shivered from the cold night air as they stared at their school from across the road. Police cruisers flooded the parking lot in response to the security alarm they'd set off when they ran out the side door. This was not part of their plan.

"Geez, Bart! We're gonna get kicked out of school for sure. And we're both 17, so we might even go to jail."

"Sean, relax! We're not going to jail. No one's even going to know it was us unless you give it away in Lab class in the morning. You know, I could've just hacked my marks if Jiggers just used the internet like every other teacher."

Sean rolled his stress marble repeatedly in his hand. "You're not worried about this, are you?"

"Not really," Bart said. "If they find out it was us, and I don't think they will, I'll call my dad and he'll take care of everything. He always does. What really bugs me, though, is that I think I left my ring in the gym change room. No one better try to steal it!"

Sean gulped. "You're worried about losing your ring when Old Man Jiggers is gonna bury us with this break-in? My parents are going to cancel my summer in Florida. I just know it."

Bart stood up and pressed the tissue on his cut hand and huffed. Now he would fail his grade and all because he couldn't find the assignments and exchange his with the class genius. "Come on, Sean. Let's get outta here before someone sees us." He pulled his car keys from his jacket and the two boys hastened in the shadows toward his father's vintage Jaguar parked two blocks away. Being rich had its perks, and Bart was used to living above everyone else. Fear had never been an option.

Yet, he was concerned that Sean's guilty conscience might break through and incriminate them both. He needed Sean to act as surprised as everyone else when they saw the huge sculpture of Jiggers' grandfather in pieces on the floor, and the smashed glass cabinet spread across the front of the classroom. Bart didn't feel remorse for his actions, but rather, was angered that Jiggers had installed a hidden security alarm in his desk that went off when Sean opened the drawer. This is what startled him and caused him to jump backwards in the first place.

The boys met by their lockers early the next morning and several female students flirted with them as they talked. One even expressed her empathy for the large bandage on Bart's hand, but they shrugged the girls off. The chattering of inquisitive students echoed in their ears as everyone talked about the disaster in Room 217.

The morning bell rang far too soon for Sean and the hallway quickly emptied. Bart and Sean sauntered into the classroom and slipped quietly into their seats.

Mr. Jiggers stood at the front of the room with a look on his face that chilled everyone. His words were sharp and it seemed as if daggers shot out from his fiery eyes. "Well, class, as you can see, someone has vandalized our lab. My grandfather's sculpture and the glass cabinet—smashed! The ant houses have been knocked over and all the ants are free. And Snake Eyes is missing."

Suddenly, the room filled with excitement as the

students began to squirm in their chairs and search for the missing snake.

Bart was the only one who appeared calm, but he was anything but calm as his heart skipped a beat in fear. His eyes shot over to the aquarium just a few feet to the right of Mr. Jiggers' desk. He was terrified of snakes, and the thought of one being loose almost paralyzed him.

"Okay everyone! Settle down!" Mr. Jiggers said. "It's obvious that this wasn't just an act of vandalism. The damage to my desk lock and the mess in my filing cabinet tells me someone was looking for something very specific."

Just then, there was a knock at the door.

"Please come in," Mr. Jiggers said. "I see you have the security video for this room."

Two security officers entered and stood at the back of the room.

Sean shifted in his chair and sweat rolled uncontrollably.

Bart cleared his throat and stared at Sean with a look that said, *Stop it!*

The boys stared at each other in shock. A security video! They hadn't seen any cameras. When was that installed? Suddenly, things didn't feel so right with them.

"This should help to identify these vandals. So, if everyone's ready, let's see that video."

All eyes stared intently at the television screen. It clearly revealed two people dressed in dark clothes and wearing black ski masks. One of them broke into Mr. Jiggers' desk, while the other one tried to open the file cabinet. When the alarm from the desk went off, the taller invader jumped sideways into the aquarium, causing him to lose his balance and fall backwards into the glass cabinet.

Several students gasped loudly as they watched the cabinet and the sculpture fall to the floor and smash.

Neither of the two characters in black said a word. Immediately, they both glanced toward the classroom door. No one came in. Then the taller character stood, wiped the blood from his cut hand caused by the broken glass and searched recklessly through the file cabinet.

The shorter one combed through the desk drawer and left it in total chaos.

The class watched as the two vandals ran out of the classroom and disappeared into the hallway. It was rather obvious that neither had taken anything.

Mr. Jiggers stopped the video and stood for a few seconds as his eerie stare ran over the body of students. "Does anyone have any idea who these two guys in black are? Bart? Can you tell us anything?"

Bart sat calmly and answered in a monotone voice. "Why are you asking me?"

"Okay, then. Maybe Sean can help. Do you know how this happened?"

Sean swallowed and shook his head. "No, I have no clue. Sorry."

Mr. Jiggers glared at the boys and then held up a signet ring. "Who owns this ring? It was found in the rubble of glass and it has an inscription on it, 'Bart the Stud'."

Bart stared at Mr. Jiggers with tongue in cheek and knew he'd been caught, but he didn't really care. He knew it would bode badly with his chemistry mark, but he wasn't going to let this little incident ruin his life. His dad was wealthy and this school's sports team existed because of his money. He wasn't worried.

Sean, on the other hand, bordered on a panic attack.

"Sean, what do you know about this?" Mr. Jiggers demanded.

Sean swallowed again and shook his head. "Why do you think I know anything about this? Could belong to anyone, but it's not mine. I don't wear a ring."

Mr. Jiggers strolled down towards Sean and leaned over him like a towering militant. He pointed to the marble that Sean was rolling nervously in his hand. "You don't know anything? Where did you get that marble, Sean?"

Sean gulped as his heart pounded so hard that it hurt his chest. He couldn't answer. He stared nervously at Mr. Jiggers whose breath fell on him like a shattered brick.

"I took this marble away from you yesterday, Sean, and it was in the top drawer of my desk when class dismissed yesterday. Now it's in your hand." Mr. Jiggers returned to the front of the classroom, quickly turned around and bellowed, "Stand up Bart Philips and Sean Roberts!"

The two boys stood slowly as some students gasped and others giggled. Everyone knew they were guilty.

Mr. Jiggers' eyes shot through them like lightning.

The room went deathly quiet.

"Explain to me, Bart, how your ring was on your finger when class ended yesterday and yet was found in the rubble of glass today. And explain to me, Sean, how the marble that was locked in my desk when class ended yesterday is now in your hand! Explain how that happened."

The sound of silence pierced the classroom.

Bart glared back at Mr. Jiggers.

Sean stood nervously as he glanced from his desk to Bart and back to his desk again.

Before either of them could speak, Mr. Jiggers held up two file folders in his hand. "Is this what you were looking for? This is your project, Bart, and this is Danny Ebb's project. It's a shame that he's away because if you had switched the contents he would have never known, and by the time he would find out, it would be too late to appeal the issue. You'd walk away with a perfect score and no one would be the wiser."

Bart clenched his jaw and stared at the teacher. He had nothing to say. It was a simple mission and he blew it. There was always Summer School to regain his grade. No worries.

Mr. Jiggers leaned against his desk. "I'm not going to press charges, but I do expect you two shameful excuses for students to pay for all the damages and replace everything that is broken. And I expect you to pay the artist to carve another sculpture."

Sean tried to compose himself and blurted out, "I'm really sorry, Mr. Jiggers. We'll talk to our dads, won't we Bart? And they'll pay for this whole thing tonight. Everything will be fixed."

The countenance on Mr. Jiggers' face changed from angry to cynical. "No, no. No parents. You boys did this and you boys will fix it... every single piece of it. It will be *your* money that pays for it, not your parents."

"Yeah, well, Mr. Jiggers, we don't have jobs so we..."

"Oh, really, Sean? Well, you do now. My

- 44 -

brother is looking for two strapping young men to help him on his dairy farm this summer. He wants to build a new barn, plough two new fields and expand the farm. I'm volunteering you two for the summer."

Sean gasped. "No," he said, "you can't do that! I'm going to Florida next week, and Bart's in a rock band and he's going to travel around. We can't do this. Our dads will pay for it."

Suddenly, a man's voice bellowed from behind them. "No, they won't!"

Bart and Sean turned and there stood both fathers, and neither wore a friendly smile.

"These boys are yours for the summer, Mr. Jiggers," Bart's father retorted. "They will work for you until every penny is paid off and until every bit of self-righteousness is worked out of them. Until I see my son become humbled and responsible, he will remain in your charge. I don't care how long it takes."

Neither Bart nor Sean had any response. Summer holidays were going to be prison for them. No vacation, no spending, no girls and no freedom. It seemed as if they had lost more than they bargained for.

Class was dismissed. The boys were ordered to clean out their lockers and prepare for their summer assignment, and Mr. Jiggers invited the entire class to gather around them and say their farewells.

Bart was determined that Mr. Jiggers' revenge ended here and that this ridiculous punishment would not humiliate him in front of his admirers.

And then he opened his locker!

***

Signs
by Autumn L. Fenton
Honorable Mention Winner 2016 Contest

Loretta Haldane flushed pink with resentment, not because the skinny teenage girl was shoplifting, but because she continued to live. She pursed her lips and waited until the girl zipped her purse with the bracelet inside. Then Loretta stomped across the worn tile floor of the campground store and bolted the entrance door from the inside. Next, she blocked the girl's path.

The girl flipped her long brown-and-blonde striped hair. "Excuse me," she said.

"You stole a bracelet," Loretta said, and folded her arms across her chest.

The girl's eyes widened, causing a tiny speck of blue glitter shadow to dislodge from her eyelid, float toward her cheek, and settle there.

Loretta turned her head away and pressed a groan down her throat. Obviously, the girl's mother needed to provide guidance in both morals and make-up application. It wasn't fair. Loretta squared her shoulders as the teenager attempted to step around her, but at five foot ten and 205 pounds, Loretta was not easy to sidestep. She patted her short gray hair and then she thrust her nose inches away from the girl's face. "Put. It. Back. Now." Loretta glanced sideways to check out her co-worker's reaction and resisted a grin at Bobbi's horrified expression.

The girl yanked the bracelet out of her purse, started to hand it to Loretta, then plunked it down on the shelf. "I'm sorry," she said. She turned toward the exit, then gasped when her elbow toppled an entire row of insect repellent. She stared at the bottles scattered across the floor, then slowly raised her head to look at Loretta. "I'm sorry," she said again.

Loretta jerked her thumb toward the door. "Get outta here."

The girl scooted around Loretta and dashed toward the locked exit.

Loretta followed her, tossing the key a few times in the palm of her hand. She unlocked the door and blocked it with her body, forcing the girl to shrink past her onto the sidewalk. "And don't you dare ever step foot in here again." Then she ambled back toward the register.

"I can't believe you locked her in," Bobbi said. She tugged a cardboard box across the counter and smoothed down the closed lid. "This might be your first day on the job, but you gotta know we just don't do stuff like that around here."

Loretta jerked the box away from Bobbi and ripped open the lid. "So what do you do when you catch someone shoplifting?"

"I never caught anyone."

"You mean you never bothered to do anything about it. Most people are too scared to act. I'm not."

Bobbi dropped her eyes and started to unload bottles of sunblock. "She's just a kid." She rolled one of the bottles in her hand and pretended to read the ingredients list.

"Kids like that grow up to be bad people."

"Aw, come on now. That's a bit extreme." Bobbi scooped a bunch of bottles from the box. One popped out of her hands and skidded across the floor. "So what do you do when your kids get outta line?"

Loretta waited until Bobbi retrieved the bottle. "I don't have any children. All three were killed when their school bus collided with a semi."

Bobbi pressed her hand against her mouth. "Oh, no! How horrible. I'm so sorry." She moved toward Loretta, arms outstretched for a hug.

"It is what it is." Loretta pivoted away from Bobbi. "So what's the best boardwalk food around here. What's this town like?"

"Boardwalk food?" Bobbi dropped her arms. "I don't know. Crab puffs, I guess. Or fries boiled in peanut oil." She lined up a bottle of sunblock next to the others. "So how long ago did they... um, you know. That's so sad. I could never handle it if something happened to my kids. What about your husband?"

"What about him? We split up after it happened. I travel in the RV. I've lived in ten states so far."

"How old were the..."

"We're not getting paid to stand around gabbing. We need to finish shelving this stuff. Our shift's nearly over." *Then I can finally do what I need to do to feel better,* Loretta thought.

The ocean mist was refreshing after the stagnant air of the campground store. It formed tiny droplets on Loretta's cheeks and hair. She inhaled long gulps of the briny air that mingled with the scent of buttery caramel popcorn and garlicky pizza. Loretta saturated her fries with so much vinegar that salt glistened from the puddles and several flopped sideways. "Whoa." She grinned at a woman behind her in line, but the woman reached for the crusty metal salt shaker without a glance.

Loretta shrugged. She weaved through the throngs of sunburned tourists to settle on a wrought iron bench facing a bank of amusement games. She watched a young father feed quarters into a Mr. Claw game. The bikini-clad mother and their tow-headed son cheered each time the metal hook almost scooped up one of the colorful plush animals, only to loosen its grip at the last second.

"So sweet," she said aloud. She winced and looked around, but no one noticed a lone, middle-aged lady talking to herself. She crossed her fingers as their shiny gold claw enclosed an orange and blue elephant, and with a jerky, robot-like movement, dropped it down into the chute.

The little family celebrated their victory with high fives and fist bumps.

Loretta clapped, too, crushing her paper cup of fries. She averted her eyes when the mother hugged the little boy. She tossed one of the fries into a flock of seagulls so she could watch them caw and dive, then wiped her palms on her khaki cargo shorts and heaved herself to her feet.

She entered a souvenir shop and rolled her eyes at the seashell dog and cat figurines. She grabbed her favorite shade of red nail polish and headed toward the check-out counter.

The sixty-something clerk sported a goatee, gold hoop earring and a magenta batik shirt.

"Those mini sewing kits---the ones by the floppy hats---you need to stick them by the register," Loretta said. "They're impulse items."

The man snapped his gum. "I'll get right on that," he said.

Loretta opened her mouth to protest the sarcasm, but shut it instead. It was almost nightfall, and she had a new bottle of *Love is Red* nail polish. She would feel better soon. She just needed to find a place.

The roads were dark and deserted outside Ocean City. Loretta explored for several miles until she found what she was looking for. She double-checked the rear view mirror to be sure no one was following before she pulled over. She backed the truck next to the yellow and black diamond-shaped sign. This one stood higher than most, so she upended a plastic milk crate on the open tailgate and balanced on that. She pulled the nail polish from her pocket, smiled at the sign, then painted a large circular nose on the buck's silhouette.

Loretta was adding the second coat of nail polish when she heard the short shrill of a police siren. She dropped her arm, but continued to face the sign as the blue and red lights flashed behind her. She twisted her mouth to one side and frowned at the sign. "This is not good, Rudolph," she said. She stepped off the milk crate and slowly rotated toward the officer. "Hi there," she said.

"Step down from the truck," he said.

"Okay, okay, just a sec. Middle-aged lady here, ya know." Loretta grinned at the officer.

"What do you think you're doing, Ma'am?"

"That should be obvious. I'm making a Rudolph, even if it is July."

"You are defacing public property. That's an unlawful act."

"Well, that's just ridiculous." Loretta scowled at him, hands on hips. "It's fun. It's whimsical."

"Defacing highway signage is an unlawful act. I need your driver's license."

"It makes people smile. Can you possibly understand a smile? You ever do that?"

"Watch your mouth, unless you want me to run you in."

Loretta sat on the edge of the tailgate, swinging her legs. She watched the stocky young officer stride to his squad car with her license. "It isn't really a joke," she whispered to his back. "It's a secret love message." Loretta dropped her head. That last night, the night they were all together for the final time, she had yelled at the children. Just for breaking a lamp.

The officer approached, carrying a clipboard and yellow forms. "Now, Ms. Haldane, explain how that happened."

"Explain?" Loretta blinked. She fanned the tears in her eyes. How could anyone explain such a tragedy?

"Ma'am. Explain how you happen to be out here in the middle of the night defacing public property."

"Oh, the sign." Loretta blotted the corner of one eye with the pad of her forefinger. "Yes, well, it's an apology and a way of connecting with my kids. They died."

The officer frowned. "An apology?"

"The night before they were killed, my children were playing Rudolph the Red-Nosed Reindeer. Beth, my oldest, painted her nose with my lipstick and made antlers with her fingers. They were all doing this silly Congo line. I screamed at them, then sent them to bed." Loretta closed her eyes for a moment. "The next day they were all dead."

The officer separated a copy of the form. "Ms. Haldane, I'm giving you a warning, only because this isn't the type of defacement that could result in a traffic accident."

"It's a Rudolph angel."

"An angel. Okay." The officer adjusted his hat. "Ms. Haldane, you really do need to move along now."

"I know." Loretta slammed the tail gate shut and climbed into the cab. She dropped the bottle of polish into the truck's cup holder.

The officer started back toward his car, then turned and came to her window. "Love is like a red, red *nose*."

Loretta widened her eyes. "Good one." She smiled. "I like it."

"Kids always know they're loved, Ma'am, even when we yell. They don't need signs." Then he tipped his hat and walked to his squad car.

She waved at him in her rear-view mirror. "Yes," she said. "Our kids always know."

***

The Red Band
by Scott Mathews
Honorable Mention Winner 2016 Contest

The head nurse warned me about Miss Murton before our visit. "Just to let you know, she's been fading in and out today. Not sure how she'll abide the dog."

My dog, Lila, and I found Miss Murton in her room just down the hall from the nurse's station.

She was working a crossword puzzle when we entered. Her silver-blue hair was in pin curls, and she wore pajama bottoms and an oversized sweat shirt with *Sunny Acres Softball* printed in bright orange.

Smiling, I knocked on her door and took a short step into the room. "Well, hello, Miss Murton. Would you like to meet my friend?"

"What?" she asked, looking up curiously as she pushed her wire framed bifocals off the tip of her nose.

"My friend," I said, gesturing to Lila at my feet. "May we come in for a visit?"

"Oh, what a cute little puppy."

With her tail wagging, Lila pulled her way to the end of the leash.

"What is it?" she asked, placing her pen and paper next to the magnifying glass on the hospital tray. "Is she your dog?"

"No, Ma'am. She's up for adoption. Lila's a Puggle, which is a cross between a pug and a beagle. We're visiting Sunny Acres today. Lila needs a chance to get out of her cage at the shelter and meet some new people."

"So, you take Lila out for a visit so she can be

free of her cage and see what the world outside is like. Is that right?" she said.

"Err… yes, Ma'am. That's right."

Miss Murton's quick response caught me off guard. Her welcoming, gentle smile belied what I believed her mental state to be. "Well, good for you, young man," she said brightly. "Good for you."

"Would you like to give Lila a treat?" I asked.

Puzzled, Miss Murton's eyes widened as she searched around the room. "Well, I'd love to, but I have nothing to give the poor little pup," she said.

"I have a bag full of treats right here in my pocket. Lila loves treats. Would you like to give her one?"

Lila's comma tail began an excited rapid thumping upon Miss Murton's leg as I unzipped the plastic bag filled with dog tidbits.

Unsure of what to do, she paused and smiled down at Lila's wagging and then at me. She seemed in that moment to be considering my question. Then, rolling up her sleeves and looking at me directly with a new sureness, she said, "No, young man. What I'd honestly like for you to do is help me get out of *my* cage." With an exaggerated sweeping gesture, she added, "Could you do that?"

"What?" I said, surprised by the earnestness of her request.

"Can you help me get out of this place?" she repeated with gentle patience.

"I'm sorry, Miss Murton," I said kindly. "You know I can't do that."

"Oh, but you can, young man. You can," she insisted, gripping Lila's collar and patting her head. "All you need to do is get me a red band." She raised her thumb and finger to illustrate. "It's about this wide and it snaps right on your wrist. You know? Like one of those hospital bracelets they give you. If I have a red band on my wrist, I can go anywhere. Any time I want," she emphasized.

"But Miss Murton, I can't. You must understand that," I said, tugging Lila away. "I'm only a volunteer. There's nothing I can do to help get you a red band."

"You don't understand, my boy," she said. "I had a red band when my daughter, Sheila, first checked me in here. She swore it was all right for me to wear one. She told the doctors and nurses it was okay. 'Of sound mind and body,' was the way she put it, and they all agreed. So, I wore one then, but not now."

"Explain how that happened."

"I went to the bank."

"What?"

"It happened when I went to the bank. Look," she sighed impatiently and continued as if explaining to a child. "I have always suspected my daughter, Sheila, was spending my money. I've always believed she was. So, I decided to leave here and go to my bank to check."

"But how'd you locate your bank?"

"That was easy. I'm not stupid. Folks around here believe I'm losing my mind. It's silly. They think I'm suffering from dementia. Slipping in and out up here," Miss Murton said, tapping her temple. "But, I'm as clear as a bell. When Sheila picks me up for lunch, we drive right by my bank. We've gone by it a thousand times. So many times that I know the way. There's a big red, white, and blue banner on the side. Why, I know it's only a few blocks away, within walking distance. I figured I could skedaddle out the front door, turn left on the sidewalk, and walk right down there to that banner before anyone missed me.

So, I did," Miss Murton said proudly.

"But, you didn't make it, did you?"

"Of course not," she said petulantly. "That fluffy young missy at the front desk has eyes like a hawk. She spied me leaving and asked where I was heading. I showed her my red band and told her a thing or two about where I could go and what I could do with it." She frowned. "I shouldn't have stopped. She didn't believe me and, before I knew it, she called up Ms. Gawd Almighty, the head nurse. We had a little tête–à–tête about the use of red bands. The how's and where's, and when's, and why's of red bands. Then, that nurse got all huffy and Sheila got a call. Next thing I know, we all got into this big deal *Inquisition* in the administrator's office, and I ended up in a twenty-four-hour lockdown. Next day, they took me off lockdown and took away my red band."

Lila, who had sprawled out on the floor by my feet, suddenly rose and started scratching behind her ear.

"Sure is a cute little thing, isn't she?" Miss Murton remarked. "She sure is a lucky dog to get out from her cage and be free. Lucky to have someone care enough to take her out for a ride to visit folks like me… in a cage like this," she finished sadly.

I nodded with a polite smile and noticed her eyes were glistening.

She hefted herself up to a more comfortable position, smoothing her oversized sweatshirt as she did. Looking over the rims of her glasses, she continued. "You know what Sheila says?" she said. "She says I'm crazy as a loon. Hallucinating. Says she's paying all her money to keep me in a nice place like this, and all I want to do is run away. I mean, can you believe it? All her money for a place like this?"

She swept about the appointed furnishings of her hospital room with outstretched arms.

Aware of her growing distress, I half stepped towards the door.

Lila's ears went up at my movement. She cocked her head from side to side and looked uncomfortably from Miss Murton to me with bulging dark eyes as if to ask if anything was wrong.

"Well, it's *my* money she's spending. It's *my* money she's paying to keep me in this cage, not hers. And, you know what? I'd rather spend my money elsewhere! Do you hear me?"

"Yes, I…"

"So, you see, young man? You really understand?" she said.

I couldn't ignore the trembling in her voice or the tears forming in her crows feet. I knew what was coming. I knew what Miss Murton wanted. She yearned for a way out of her cage. Freedom. And there was nothing I could do about it. An uneasy silence filled the room as I bent to pick up Lila and turned to leave.

"I need to get out. I need a red band," she said. "Need to get to the bank to get my money. Need a red band so I can go down the street to the bank and get my money. So, I can get free. Don't you see?"

"I'll… see what I can do," I said. With the dog in my arms, I turned once more to her pleading eyes and quietly left the room.

At the nurse's station down the hall, I asked how I could get an appointment with the administrator.

***

The Hourglass
by Deborah Owen
CEO, Creative Writing Institute

The thought hit her upside the head with such force that it stunned her for a full moment. She stared at the toast in her hand, only half buttered, as the simple question rolled in her mind like a tumbleweed without bounds. The question had no apparent answer, but the longer she puzzled over it, the bigger it became. The question was… when did she quit burning the toast?

It seemed like only yesterday that she married and moved out of state, discovered coleslaw was made from cabbage and not lettuce, invented wiener gravy to fill hungry tummies, and the earth wouldn't spin off its axis if she didn't measure ingredients precisely.

Chrissy laid the toast aside and allowed the house slippers to slap the floor as she ambled to the bathroom mirror. That reflection couldn't be hers. She traced the wrinkles on her face, pulled the skin up until it was smooth, then allowed it to fall again. Wrinkles rained like a flood eroding a steep hillside.

Grey hairs stood out in rebellion. She patted them down. They popped back up. Oh, well. Hair dye covered most of them. She fingered the bottle of color. When did she first use color? Twenty years ago? No, more than that. Or was it less?

She powdered her face, turned sideways and frowned at her sagging bust. Definitive waist bulges replaced yester-decades rolling curves.

She sighed and sank onto the commode fully dressed, elbows on knees.

"Chrissy? Where are you? Chrissy?" Lumbering

old feet scooted over the carpet and down the hall. "Is my toast ready? Where'd you get to, woman?"

Charlie stood staring at her. She looked up.

"What in the world… ? Pottying with your clothes on now?" he said with the usual laugh.

When didn't he laugh? She didn't have one to return, but he still had the most beautiful brown eyes. When did her handsome, dashing young man turn into a stalwart gent with trifocals, false teeth and two chins?

"What's the matter, honey? What'cha doin' sittin' there like that?"

His voice failed to reach the part of her mind that now visualized an hourglass with fast-leaking sand. The sand was running out. She should turn it over and let it start again, but what was the point? It would only leak out again, and each time she turned it, it leaked even faster. Was Charlie totally unaware of this, her latest discovery? The new truth rocked her soul. Stole her breath. Made her want to cry. Her eyes touched his and she spoke with a soft voice, like a kindergartener asking her first question in school. "When did we get old, Charlie?"

He paused, and the habitual smile melted. His face softened, and he placed the back of a rough finger on her cheek. "We're not old, honey. We're just… mature."

Her eyes bugged and she glanced around to see if anyone could hear. No, they were alone. Very alone. Was it safe to mention such things aloud? She would try. "I never saw the hourglass, Charlie. Not until just now. One day I was pregnant with Ronnie, and a few weeks later he was graduating from high school. A few more weeks and Ronnie graduated from college, and a few more and he was married. And just when I was beginning to adjust, the grandchildren came, and I love them with all my heart, but I can't have them all the time and now they're leaving, too… don't you see? The hourglass did it. It always flips over and each time I flip it, it runs out even faster until I can't make sense of it anymore."

"Can't make sense of what, honey?"

Maybe he knew it shouldn't be discussed aloud. That had to be it. She motioned to him with one finger, rolling her eyes. "Come closer," she said. "I don't want anyone to hear."

Charlie frowned. "Nobody's here but you and me, Chrissy."

"Shhh… listen. Can't you hear the sand in the hourglass? I know you do. Why didn't you tell me?"

"Tell you what, honey? Are you feeling okay?"

"It's a thief! The hourglass is a thief. It stole from me. It stole everything I ever had, and now look at what's left." She put a hand to her face. Her voice rose with every word. She walked to the mirror and looked at Charlie through it. "See? See what the hourglass did when I wasn't looking?" She pointed at her reflection. "Explain how that happened, Charlie. Please – explain that to me."

"C'mon, honey. Everything's going to be fine," he said.

"Fine?" Her voice rose. "We're standing here looking like the living dead and you say we're fine?"

"You're making too much out of this, Chrissy. Everyone ages. You're still beautiful." He stepped closer and looked at her through the mirror.

Her eyes widened, as though she could see something he couldn't see, hear something he couldn't hear. Chrissy turned around, her eyes darting around in panic. "You don't know, do you? You can't see what it's done to us. It's deprived you of your ability to reason as well. Look at me, Charlie. LOOK AT ME! Don't you see what it's done to me? What it's done to you?" She grabbed his shirt with both hands and tried to shake him.

Charlie placed kind hands on her shoulders. "Come on now. You're getting way too serious, honey. That last birthday threw you for a loop, huh?" He strained to bring up a little chuckle.

His chuckle jolted her. Her pale neck reddened and a flush filled her cheeks. Quite suddenly, she stood stick straight, like a proud politician. She smoothed her clothing, looked up at him and said, "Move."

"You want to move? Or are you talking about Ronnie moving to California? Or maybe you want me to move out." He laughed at his own jokes, but the jesting was laborious.

She raised her chin, wishing she could meet his eyes on his level, but the six-foot hulk towered over her. Her eyes glazed and turned to ice. Speaking as though she could barely keep from slitting his throat and sending his body to a science lab in Yugoslavia, she said, "Move… your… hands… off… my… shoulders. Is that plain enough?"

The smile drained from his face and left him ashen. Charlie raised his hands in surrender and backed into the hall. Before he could say another word, Chrissy slammed the door so hard the windows rattled. "Now, that's enough of that," he said with rising anger. He grabbed the handle and twisted, but to no avail. It was locked. "Come out of there!" He waited for the response that failed to come. "Do you hear me?" He banged on the door with his fist. "Open this door, Chrissy. Chrissy! Do you have your hearing

aids in? Do you hear me? Open this door right now."
He shook it with all his might.

His slippers scuffed the hall carpet as he paced,
wiped a hand over the top of his head and then down
over his face, ending on his chin. There he stood,
suddenly very tired. He leaned into the corner and
rubbed his eyes. Red eyes. Eyes that brimmed with
moisture. Eyes that turned into the corner to unload
their secret, and there he stood, like a little boy being
punished at school.

The old grey schnauzer nuzzled him. "It's my
fault," he said to Trixie, who tilted her head in concern
and whined. "Always trying to make her laugh when I
should just leave her be." Charlie swiped the back of
his hand across his eyes, bent down and scratched the
dog's ears.

She whined.

"Now don't you start crying, too."

Trixie wagged her stub of a tail.

"Everything's gonna be all right. Where's your
ball? Hmm? Go find it, girl. Go find your ball." Trixie
limped away.

Charlie stared after her, and when she rounded
the corner, he looked up and said, "Well, Lord. I
expect all three of us are just about ready." He tried
the bathroom door again. Still locked. He knocked.
"Christine? I'm sorry I got mad. Open the door,
honey. Please?" He put his ear to the door and heard
her singing in the shower. Singing? He listened again.
Yup. Singing. At least she was okay. Charlie chose the
closest chair to hold his body and kept his eye on the
bathroom door.

In due time, the shower stopped and the toilet
flushed. The medicine cabinet door closed a couple of
times and Chrissy continued to warble. Charlie mused

on the years she sang for church services, back in the day when they could go. What a voice. What in thunder was that woman doing in there! An hour later, the lock turned on the door. She peered through the crack and he smiled. "There's my little beauty queen," he said with the customary booming voice.

She opened the door wider, almost with shyness, and stood as tall as her 5'1" frame would allow. Her blouse was buttoned straight and tucked in nice and neat. Red hair lay neatly combed. Her face blossomed a little too loud with blush. She batted mascara-laden eyes.

Their smiles met and he stood to greet her. "You're beautiful," he said.

She stared at his lips.

"Why wouldn't you open the door?" he said

She stared in obvious confusion. "You're a big boy. You could've opened it."

"I couldn't. You locked it."

"I did?" she said.

"Yes. I yelled for you to open it. You had me scared."

"I didn't hear you." She put both hands up to her ears. Puddles leaped into her eyes, wrinkles draped her brow and despair stretched across her mouth. "I don't have my hearing aids on."

Her eyes opened so wide that he thought she was about to scream.

"I wear hearing aids, don't I? Don't I?" she said. "Don't you see what's happening? I wear hearing aids! Doesn't that tell you something?" She backed up, hands still on her ears.

"Yes, it tells me you've been lipreading all day. I thought that was a thing of the past since they made those special things that help a little. Come here, honey. Sit in my chair for a minute. I'll get 'em."

When he returned, Chrissy sat like a statue, staring at her hands, tears dripping off her face.

Charlie pulled the footstool up and collapsed on it with a groan. "Here, here now. What are you crying about? Huh? Aren't I taking good care of you? Here, let me put these in for ya. Let's see… this one's for the right ear. Yup. That fits. Well, this one must be for the left ear then, unless you've got another ear I don't know about," he said with a snicker. He pulled his handkerchief out and dabbed the mascara streaks on her face. "Oh, my. Those black streaks make you look like a zebra, but it so happens I always wanted a zebra. You are my sunshine, do you know that?" he said, tipping her chin up with one finger. He continued mopping her face. "My sunshine, my only sunshine… you make me happy when skies are grey. You'll never know, dear, how much I love you… please don't take my sunshine away."

She smiled and his heart smiled.

"We love that song, don't we Chrissy? That's our song."

Chrissy nodded. "Tell me again. How long have we been married?" she said.

"Sixty-seven years, my darling. Now, tell me what happened a while ago. You know – with all the yelling and…"

"I didn't yell," she said.

"What? You went crazy in there! You yelled at me and locked me out. I tried the door, but…"

"It must have been someone else. I didn't yell," she said with quiet determination.

Charlie pulled her over to him, kissed her hair and smelled the fresh shampoo, and another fragrance wound around in his brain until he finally put a name to it. *Seven Winds perfume. My favorite. She wore it when we dated. And she still has some?* He held her tight. Her arms looped around his big waist and there they sat. How long had it been since they hugged like that? Tears rose unbidden and he swiped the hankie across his eyes.

"Well, we better get breakfast, my love."

A fearful look crossed her face.

"C'mon now. Everything's just fine," he said. "Let me help ya up, if I can get up m'self, that is. My old body doesn't bend like it used to." He stood and pulled her up. A smile lit his face. "Just look at you. You're downright gorgeous. Did you get all prettied up just for me?"

Chrissy's smile bloomed and she nodded.

"And I recognize that sexy perfume, young lady. Are you sure you aren't trying to seduce me?"

Chrissy giggled.

"Would you do me the honor of accompanying me on a date tonight, beautiful lady?"

A giggle rippled to the surface. "I would be pleased to accompany you, kind sir."

He looped her hand in his arm. "Did you make my toast?" he said, patting her hand as they walked to the kitchen.

A cloud crossed her eyes as she shuffled along. "Yes, but it's cold now. And I don't think I got it all buttered. I got to thinking about something else. Something real important, but I can't remember now what it was. And then I went into the bathroom and…"

"Don't you be worryin' about cold toast half-buttered," he said, deliberately interrupting. We'll drink hot orange juice to make up for it." Chrissy took her seat and Charlie laid the half-buttered toast on his side of the table, poured their juice, and sat down.

"Where's my toast?" she said with a forlorn stare.

He stopped, toast poised halfway to his mouth. "You already ate it, honey."

"No, I didn't."

"You always eat your toast before I get up."

With the look of a cornered mouse, she shrugged and said, "Well, that's not very nice of me. I should've waited to eat with you."

"That's okay. I don't mind a bit. Hold on. Be right back. I forgot to give Trixie some water and her bowl's empty. Now you stay right there," he said.

"Okay. I'm planted."

Chrissy could hear the water run and the clink of the bowl. She sipped orange juice and spun it 'round and 'round in the little circle of sweat beneath it. Tiny bubbles rose to the surface and popped. An endless amusement for those who wait.

Charlie made his way back to the table and picked up his toast.

"Charlie?"

"Hmm?"

"Why did you only butter half of your toast?"

His eyes squinted a little. "But… you…" He froze as a thought entered his head.

Sometimes it might be a good idea to just humor her, the doctor said.

Charlie's eyes puddled.

"Did I say something wrong?" Chrissy said.

"Wrong? No, no. I just have a spec in my eye." He pulled his hankie, put on the proper show and then blew his nose. "There. All better now," he said.

"You should've let me make it," Chrissy said.

"Make what?"

"Your toast. I would have buttered all of it for you."

He wrapped a thin, veined hand around hers. "Don't you worry about a thing. It's fine. Just fine. You can make it next time. Hey – I have a brilliant idea. Let's have some excitement today. Let's take Trixie to the park and we'll feed the pigeons. Then we'll stop by Baskin-Robbins and you can have anything you want."

"Oh, I'd love it," she said. "We haven't done that in such a long time, but…"

"But what?"

"Can we afford it?"

"You bet," he said. "Get anything you want!"

"Oh, my. I need to think about that. And I need to put make-up on and comb my hair. I want to be pretty for our date."

"Don't worry about make-up. You're as beautiful as the first day we met, and you can't improve on perfection." He winked.

Chrissy laughed out loud. "I can't wait to feed the pigeons. I have to hurry. Let's see. I think I'll wear my green slacks and that blouse you like so well."

"You have the green slacks on, honey."

She looked down, and surprise sprang on her face. "Well, so I do. I'll just change my blouse then and fix my make-up." Chrissy pushed her chair back and shuffled to the living room, talking to herself. "I wonder what kind of ice cream I should get. It's been such a long time since we went to…" Her voice dwindled in the distance.

Charlie laid the half-buttered, cold toast down and stared at it. Then he looked up and folded his hands. "Thank you, Lord, for all the years we've had together. They've been good ones… for the most part."

Trixie laid her head on his lap and whined.

Charlie paused to stroke her head. "And thank you for Trixie, too, Lord. And don't forget, when that time comes, we'd all like to travel together. Amen."

***

BIO: Deborah Owen is the CEO and founder of Creative Writing Institute. CWI provides a variety of writing courses with personal tutors and is a 501(c)3 nonprofit charity that offers free writing courses to cancer survivors. Deborah won Honorable Mention over 16,000 entries in a Writer's Digest short story contest and has had many articles accepted for publication. She loves God, her family and Kettle potato chips.

Just Kidding
by Jianna Higgins
Coordinating Judge & Award Winning Author

Ruby Smith paused mid-corridor and leaned on her walking frame. "Hey, Gidget," she said with a snort. "Have you put on weight?"

The short, sturdy woman swiveled to face her. "Mrs. Smith! Do *not* call me that. You'll refer to me as Nurse Piggott."

Ruby giggled behind a gnarled hand. This woman was always fun to poke. "Really? You'd rather be called Miss Piggy?"

"Mrs. Smith, my name is Bridget Piggott, and as the Sorrento Retirement Facility manager, I deserve your respect."

"Just kidding, Gidget. Keep your hair on or you'll blow a fuse." She wasn't kidding. The woman was round as a barrel and sported a broad, turned-up nose.

Bridget's body stiffened and her mouth tightened. "Speaking of hair… I see you dyed yours again. That is a very intense shade of blue. I've been informed that your bathroom basin is now streaked in multiple colors. Explain how that happened." She stepped toward Ruby's bedroom door.

"My basin is still white, so the snitch must be color blind," Ruby said and moved to block her. "Don't you go in my room or I'll scream so loud your ears will die. I don't want your bad energy where I sleep. I'll have nightmares."

"Arrgh." Red blotches climbed up Bridget's neck and flooded her cheeks. "You, Mrs. Smith, are the nightmare, and you're going to regret coming to live here. Mark my words."

Ruby's smile grew wide like a Cheshire cat and she wagged her finger. "No, Miss Piggy, mark mine. I'm a fee-paying resident. You only work here which means that you're disposable." She pushed her walking frame back and forth across the carpet as she waited for the manager's retort.

Bridget's scrunched face made her nasal breathing sound like a bull about to charge. Ready to pounce in Ruby's direction, she turned at the sound of approaching footsteps. "Ah, Nurse Moth, I had another resignation today, effective immediately, so you'll have to fill in on your day off."

Ruby tapped one foot at the facility manager's sudden change of focus. Sparring was fun, and she didn't want to be interrupted.

Melanie Moth came to a sudden halt. "But I have plans to work at the homeless shelter tomorrow," she said. "And I haven't had any time off in four weeks. Staff keep leaving."

"Don't whine if you want to retain your position as head nurse on this wing. You'll do as I say or you'll be looking for a new job."

Melanie swiped her arm across her forehead and blinked weary eyes. "Fine. I'll be in tomorrow."

"See that you are." Bridget marched away toward the entrance doors.

Irritated at the loss of her prey, Ruby cupped her hands around her mouth. "See ya, Miss Piggy."

"Shhh," Melanie said, her eyes glued to the woman's retreating back. "She might come back."

Ruby raised her eyebrows. "What? You're afraid of her? You need a spine transplant." She shook her head.

Melanie sagged in relief as Bridget turned the corner. "If you were smart, you'd be afraid, too."

I'm surrounded by nincompoops, Ruby thought. "You're an oxygen thief, Nurse Moth. Just like Gidget. Stay out of *my* oxygen zone or you'll suck the life out of me." She pushed her walker toward the entrance doors to check on the state of the sky.

"Why're you so mean?"

Ruby paused and called over her shoulder. "Gotta get my kicks somehow. This place is as boring as your blonde hair."

Melanie patted her tightly pinned bun and then pulled her hand away. "I noticed your latest *friend* abandoned you. Have you ever wondered why?"

Although that was true, it was no cause for alarm. Ruby was never alone for long. "No, smarty pants. My personality is way too big for most people to handle. Now get about your work before I report you to your Kommandant." She said the last word with a German accent. Ruby veered back to her bedroom and closed the door behind her. She glanced around at the stark white walls, white curtains, white bedspread and blonde oak dresser. Stepping in front of the mirror, she gave a low groan as she pulled at her blue hair. "I'm the only bright light hovering around this dull joint."

At lunchtime, Ruby sat with Rosa and Arnie De Luca and Barney Baldwin. When Bridget walked past carrying a loaded plate of pot roast and vegetables, Ruby called, "Miss Piggy, you should be eating fresh air and exercise or you're gonna crack our floor when you walk." She watched the steam from the nurse's food curl into the air and pretended it came from her ears.

Bridget stopped, set her plate on the table and

placed her hands on her hips. "I've decided that Sorrento is unable to meet your needs, Mrs. Smith. You're being transferred to Twin Oaks nursing home."

Uh oh. Backfire. Ruby dropped her fork and it clattered across the table and onto the floor. "You can't do that!"

Bridget jiggled on the spot as though fluffing her feathers. "Oh, I assure you I can. I'd move you to Timbuktu if I knew where it was."

"It's in West Africa," Barney said through a mouthful of mashed potato.

Bridget's eyes lit up. "Perfect. Thank you, Mr. Baldwin. I see your false eye is slightly askew. Kindly go and fix it. People don't want to see that while they eat." She marched out of the lounge cradling her plate of food.

Ruby's pulse escalated and her lungs felt squeezed. "Barney, she can't send me to Timbuktu, can she?" She tried not to stare at his false eye as it gazed off to the right.

"No, she can't. But it sounds like she has the authority to transfer you out of here."

Ruby felt wobbly in her tummy and she had barely eaten two mouthfuls. "Do you want to sit with me at dinner tonight? Just the two of us?"

Barney scraped his fork around his plate chasing wayward peas. "No thanks. You auditioned me as a boyfriend last Monday. Remember? You were bored with my jokes after two minutes."

Ruby didn't usually give second chances, but she liked Barney. "Want to try again with a new joke?"

"Right now?"

"Sure, why wait for dinner when you can woo me now."

Barney coughed into his hand. "Okay. Uh... a businessman traveling to New York for the first time called ahead to check the hotel facilities because his doctor put him on an exercise program. *'Hello, can you tell me if you have a weight room?'* he said. *'No,'* said the receptionist, *'we have a lobby. You can wait there.'* Was that funny?" He spread a hopeful grin.

Ruby sighed. She had chatted up all the single men, and none of them could cut it. "Sorry, Barney, you'll have to do better than that. No offence."

"None taken. I just don't have what it takes to entertain you."

"That's okay. We're still friends."

After lunch, Ruby sat on a couch and stared out the lounge window at two male ducks poking each other with their beaks. *I want someone to poke. I'm so bored.* She heard Melanie's voice approaching and slid down in her seat to hide her blue hair.

"This is the lounge, Mrs. Jefferson. You can watch TV, borrow library books and magazines, or play board games and cards at the other end."

"Oh, honey, it's lovely. I think I'm going to like living here."

Someone new? Ruby wriggled around onto her knees, lost her balance and face planted into the soft cushions. She used her strong arm to push herself up and peeped over the top of the couch. "Hi. I'm Ruby. You won't know anyone here, so you can have dinner with me. I'll look after you."

Melanie's eyes widened, and she stood in front of the woman as if to protect her. "Now, Mrs. Smith, I'm sure Mrs. Jefferson wants to take things easy on her first day."

The woman smiled and shook her head. "Thank you, Nurse Moth, but I think it's a lovely idea. I'd be delighted to have dinner with you, Ruby. My name is Grace Jefferson and I love your bright blue hair. I wish I had the nerve to do something so… exciting."

Ruby stood and pushed her walker toward Grace. "Thank you. I'm trying different colors until I find one that suits my personality. Blue's not a winner. It doesn't say enough about me."

"I can already tell," Grace said.

Ruby caught Melanie's smirk. What would she know? "Don't you laugh at me Nurse Mealy-Mouth. You and I are at different ends of the personality spectrum, and I know which end I prefer."

Melanie stared at the floor before she rushed from the lounge.

"That was a bit harsh, wasn't it? She has a difficult job."

Ruby noted the concern on her face as she watched the nurse leave the room. Concern for Melanie? "Don't worry about her. She can hold her own. Come on, it's a bit early, but we can get a table and check out the single men. It's slim pickings, but new ones come in all the time." Ruby showed Grace to her usual table and parked her walking frame. "So what's your story? Don't tell me your dead husband's name was Thomas Jefferson or I'll wet my pants. You're still on probation as a friend."

Grace gave her a serene look. "First of all, Ruby," she said, "my husband's name *was* Thomas Jefferson, but I prefer to call him *Tom* rather than my *dead* husband. Second, I also get to choose my friends, and you, too, are on probation."

Ruby gaped with an open mouth, snapped it shut, then slapped her knee. "Well, flip my switch. There's finally somebody in here with a bit of gumption." So many people were drawn toward Ruby, mostly as spectators. She could no longer conduct a large circle of hangers-on as in the old days, but having one friend would be nice, and the position was vacant. *Play it safe. Change the subject.* "Have you met the center manager, Gidget Piggy?"

"That's her name? How unfortunate. I think I saw her when I arrived. Short lady, rather well built, loud voice. She was yelling at someone with long, curly red hair."

"Yeah, that's Rochelle, a nurse aide. She sasses me sometimes, but she's a decent kid. Only Gidget, Melanie and Rochelle have stuck around. Staff leave Sorrento like rats off an exploding bomb. I wish the nurses would take a hike as well. Just keep a cook, dishwasher and a janitor and we can run the place ourselves," Ruby cackled.

Two hours later when Ruby returned from her afternoon nap, she found Grace sitting outside on a wooden bench. "Hey, it's quite warm out here. Thanksgiving's in a few weeks. I thought it'd be cold."

Grace's mouth dropped open. "Wow, you work fast!"

"Sure do." Ruby turned her head from side to side. "How do you like it?"

"I've never seen such siren red hair. It does a good job of announcing you."

"Yes, I like it, but it's not a winner," Ruby said. "Hey, why siren?"

"No man in a hundred miles is going to miss it. In fact, I think a blind man could see you coming."

Ruby slapped her knee. "That's the plan. Girlfriends are okay, but I need me some lovin'. Know what I mean?"

"I'm fairly sure I do."

Ruby nodded. "Hey, guess what. Gidget's transferring me to Twin Oaks for being a naughty girl. I don't know how to stop her, Grace. I might've outsmarted myself this time."

"I'm sorry about that, Ruby. I'm enjoying our trial friendship. Actually, I nearly went to Twin Oaks. I just had a stronger feeling about this place."

"Well, you should've gone there. Then when *I* get there, we could meet for the first time, and I wouldn't say something dumb about your husband."

Grace raised one eyebrow and a corner of her mouth quirked up.

"Yeah, just kidding. I would've said it, but we'd still be friends just like we are now. I don't want to go there," she said in a rare, solemn moment. "Hey, I know. I'll follow Gidget around like Magnum P.I. Now that was a hunk of man flesh… especially with his shirt off."

"Ruby, please."

"Oh, don't be a prude. You slept with your husband, so… you know. Anyway, Gidget's crazy as all get out, and folks like that have abnormal vices. I just need to learn what hers is. I'm crazy, and my vice is men, so I know what I'm talking about."

At noon the following day, Ruby shuffled along the corridor following the smell of pot pie on the air. Bridget grabbed her shoulder with talons that clawed at Ruby's frail skin. "Ow, let go. You aren't allowed to do physical abuse on me. I bruise easy."

Nurse Piggott swallowed and scanned the corridor to check who might be listening. "I was just getting your attention because every time I turn around, there you are. It's as if you're stalking me."

Ruby sucked in her bottom lip. Hunger was currently driving her to the dining room instead of her stakeout. "Hey! I stalk men, and I'm not bent, lady. No offense if *you* are bent, but I think *you're* following me... like right now. You need to stop, or I'll sue for harassment."

Bridget pursed her lips but walked away muttering, "Breathe. She'll soon be gone. Just focus and breathe."

Ruby followed her to the staffroom, took a quick look around the corner, and then pulled back and leaned against the wall, thankful for good hearing.

"I bring my own plunger coffee in this thermos," Bridget said. "I can't drink that instant rubbish."

"Why not? We have to drink it," Melanie said.

"Can't you think for yourself, Nurse Moth? Perhaps you aren't head nurse material after all. I'll need to keep a closer eye on you."

Rochelle added, "The residents have to drink it, too. Why not get them a proper coffee machine. They pay enough to stay here."

"Mind your business, child, if you want to keep your job. I have better things to spend my discretionary budget on than decent coffee."

Ruby peered around the corner again.

At that moment, Bridget, with her back to Melanie and Rochelle, slipped a hip flask from her pocket and poured golden brown liquid into her coffee cup.

"Gotcha," Ruby muttered and motored off to lunch, unable to form a plan on an empty stomach. She paused at the dining room doors and surveyed the sea of white and silver hair. Unable to spot Grace, she planted herself at Rosa and Arnie De Luca's table. "Hello, people. How're ya doin'? So Arnie, you still happy with Rosa, or are you maybe looking to trade up?"

Rosa laughed. "Ruby, are you hitting on my man?"

"Just kidding. I don't poach husbands, but I've been on my own too long." When Grace entered the room Ruby smiled… until she took a seat next to Barney Baldwin.

Thirty minutes later, fueled with coffee, protein and carbs, Ruby weaved her way to the east wing and checked the lounge.

The man sat hunched in his wheelchair staring into space. His craggy face was barely visible under a faded cap, stitched with the words, Smurf: Specialist Locksmith. Nasal prongs poked up his nose and the attached tubing flowed down to an oxygen bottle.

"Hey, Smurf."

He looked up through bushy white eyebrows and adjusted his smeared glasses. "Ruby… that you?"

"Yeah. I need to borrow your lock pick kit."

"No kiss hello?"

Ruby stayed just out of his arm's reach. "Not if you paid me ten million dollars."

"Come on, for old time's sake," he pouted.

"Drop it, Smurf. Ain't gonna happen."

He licked his lips. "You know I've always been in love with you."

Ruby rolled her eyes. "Yeah… you and half the male population."

Smurf scratched at his scraggly beard. "Every time I heard you got divorced, you'd already got yourself married again. Are you out of husbands right now?"

"My fifth husband, Alfie, died of a heart attack a year ago."

His dull eyes came alive and danced with mirth. "Well, gorgeous, here I am," he said with a stained, false-teeth smile.

"Look, Smurf, I'm looking, but I have to be in love. Sorry, but you just don't do it for me. So where's your lock pick kit?"

"Shhh… the walls have ears," he said.

A nurse swished into the room out of nowhere. "Seamus Murphy, you don't own such a thing, do you?"

He gave her his *innocent of the crime* face. He mouth to Ruby, *See what I mean?* "Of course not. She was just kidding."

The woman was dressed in the same uniform as Melanie Moth and for once, Ruby was speechless.

"I thought you were the best burglar in the business," the nurse said. She didn't wait for a reply and turned to Ruby. "Hello, I'm Ingrid, nurse manager on this wing. I love your hair. It's like fire engine red on steroids. Where do you live?"

Ruby shuffled her feet. The nurse had caught them, but she didn't seem too bothered. "West wing. One of Melanie's inmates."

"Well, nice to meet you. Watch out for this one." Ingrid flicked a thumb at Smurf. "He's incorrigible. I'll be back to change your oxygen tubing, Smurf."

Ruby craned her neck around the door and down the hall. "So, can I borrow it?"

"What're you planning on stealing?"

"Not stealing. Just gonna take out the trash. Hurry up! Hand it over."

"You're the bossiest she-devil I ever knowed. All right, here it is. Just get it back to me fast." He reached an age-spotted hand into his pocket and handed the kit to Ruby.

The next morning, Ruby dawdled into breakfast,

yawning. Sleep had eluded her and she visited the bathroom five times for a change of scenery. She lifted each lid of the silver serving dishes and sighed. Cumulatively, there was not enough to feed one sparrow. She pushed the kitchen swing doors open and called, "Cook! Bacon and eggs with a side of hash browns. Any time is good, but three minutes would be about right." When Cook nodded, Ruby took her usual seat.

"You've outdone yourself this time," Grace said. "You look like a green traffic light. Go! Yes, it suits you. It's my favorite so far."

Ruby patted her hair and crinkled her nose. The new dye job hadn't lived up to expectations. She liked it when she went to bed, but in the harsh light of morning, her heart missed a beat when she caught her reflection in the mirror. "I like the *go* part, but it's not a winner either. I think I look more like a Granny Smith apple. I've asked my accomplice to poach another color. I have a good feeling about the next one."

"Poach? No, don't tell me. Ignorance is bliss."

Ruby tapped her fingers against her chin. "Speaking of getting into trouble, Grace, you gotta help me get rid of Gidget or you're gonna be minus one trial friendship."

"Nurse Piggott?"

"Yeah, that's what I said… Miss Piggy. She's a menace to society." Ruby watched, amused, as Grace's eyes widened.

Cook blasted through the swinging doors and set Ruby's food on the table before her. The smell of crispy bacon sent her taste buds into rapture. "Hey Cook. What's your real name?"

Cook froze with her hands midair. "I like to be

called *Cook*. Ain't nobody allowed to call me Jehoshaphina. Whatever was my mother thinking?" She marched away muttering under her breath.

Ruby shook her head. *Jehosha… what?* The name rang a bell but she had no idea why.

Grace leaned forward and spoke in a low voice. "You're planning to, uh, knock off Nurse Piggott? Honey, I can't be involved in any criminal activities."

"At our age, it's only semi-illegal, and like you say, if you don't know the details, you'll be fine. I just need some backup."

"I'll only help if it's to keep you safe."

"If I get caught, Gidget will actually kill me dead."

Grace munched her toast, deep in thought. "What would I have to do?"

"Easy peasy lemon squeezy. Just stand next to the big window near the end of the corridor and keep an eye out for Gidget coming toward her office. If you see her, have a coughing fit."

Grace bit her bottom lip and then smiled. "Well, okay. I haven't done anything naughty for at least sixty years. Promise you won't hurt her."

Hmm, that was a tough call. "I won't touch her. Just gonna serve up a dish of cold justice."

With a full stomach, Ruby left her walking frame with Grace and used the wall for support as she negotiated the corridor and turned the corner. She pulled out the lock picks and opened the office door in seconds. "Piece of cake. Who says I've got dementia?" she said under her breath.

The manager's purse sat on the floor beneath the desk. When Ruby reached for it, she lost her balance and tumbled to the floor. *Oh no! What a place to break a hip.* She tipped onto one buttock and then the other. *Ouch. That smarts, but my butt… is fine.* She chuckled at her intended pun. She located the two items she sought in the monstrous purse and began Mission: Phase One. As she pulled on the side of the desk to get to her feet again, she heard voices. *Oops. Out of time.* Ruby lay on her side and curled into a fetal position. When the office door burst open, she heard Grace coughing. *Thanks Grace, but 'better late than never' doesn't apply here.*

"The sooner that Smith woman is gone, the happier I'll be," Bridget said. "Should be any day now."

"Are you sure this is legal?" Melanie said.

"She's diagnosed with dementia, although I've only noticed age-related cognitive decline, but nevertheless, it works in my favor. She's not deemed to have capacity which gives me the authority. Won't you be glad when she's gone? She makes you look like a gormless idiot every day."

Melanie drew in a slow breath. "I'll be glad not to put up with her constant snipes, but she can be amusing for the other residents."

"Right. At your expense. Phone Twin Oaks and check on the availability of rooms."

"Yes, of course."

Ruby peeked under the back of the desk and just for a moment she made eye contact with Melanie. *Uh oh. Here it comes. Payback time.* She stuffed the lock pick kit into a pocket and struggled for a plausible reason to be hiding under the desk.

Bridget continued, "I wish that Smith woman and I were circles on a Venn diagram that never intersected again."

As if she held a wand that sprinkled fairy dust, Ruby flicked her wrist in Bridget's direction. "Wish granted," she mouthed.

"If there's nothing else," Melanie said, "I'll make that call to Twin Oaks and you might get your wish."

Bingo! Ruby thought. *But only one of us will get our wish, and my money's on me.*

"Yes, yes, go ahead. I'll be at a meeting for the next hour, but I'll be back for afternoon tea. Try to keep the place running smoothly."

Ruby caught the smirk on Melanie's face before she swished out of the office. *Why didn't she tell Gidget on me?* she wondered. She looked under the desk at the nurse manager's chubby legs and stiffened. The woman was walking around the side of the desk. Ruby scooted to the back of the desk, aware that her backside was showing if anyone came to the door.

Bridget pulled out her chair and the air whooshed from its cushion as she sat. "Ahhh, that's better," she said and kicked off her pumps.

Ruby could almost see the sour odor as it wafted up her nose. *How don't her feet know I'm allergic to stinky smells*, she thought as she felt the familiar tickle that preceded a sneeze. Her eyes watered. She held her breath. She squeezed her nose. Nothing worked. It was coming like a freight train and there was no stopping it. She sucked in her breath once, twice, three times. Ruby clapped a hand over her nose and mouth to muffle the sound, but out it came... aaahhh choooo!

Bridget slapped both hands on her wooden desk. "Who's in my office?" As she stood, her chair shot backward and slammed into the wall.

This is it. She'll snap my neck and roll me out in a laundry hamper. I always wanted to ride in one, but I'd rather do it alive.

At that moment the phone rang loud enough to

wake a mummy in Egypt.

Slipping on her shoes, Bridget ignored it. "If there's someone in here, I'll find you." She ripped open tall, thin cupboard doors. "Argghh," she shouted. "I know I heard someone sneeze."

Ruby could see the woman's shoes as they swiveled in a circle. The phone continued to jangle.

"All right, all right," Bridget said and grabbed the receiver. "Yes! Oh, Twin Oaks. She can come tomorrow? I'll be… I mean *she'll* be thrilled. Mrs. Smith? Oh, she's a sweet lady. You'll adore her. Goodbye." Bridget dropped the receiver and clapped her hands. "Twin Oaks, you'll never be the same again." She removed an item from her desk and moved over to the door before looking back. "Hmm, maybe I was hearing things… just excitement. Yes, must be." She popped in the button on the door handle, stepped outside and pulled it shut.

Ruby's heart thumped like a drum. "Phew, I'm too old for this kind of excitement," she muttered. "Now, how did I get down here, and how do I get back up?" She used her strong arm and leg to get out from under the desk, maneuvered her leg under her bottom and pulled herself onto her knees. "Good. Phase one… complete the mission… check. Phase two… get up and leave… never gonna happen." Ruby crawled over to the door, cracked it open and peered out with one eye. "Coast clear. Tally ho." After several torturous minutes and carpet-burned knees, Ruby reached the corner and sighed with relief. She gave a low whistle and Grace hurried toward her.

"I nearly had heart failure when those two nurses went around the corner. I expected the police to arrive and haul you away in a squad car," Grace said. "How in the world did you not get caught?"

"I hid under Gidget's desk."

"They didn't see you?"

Ruby remembered Melanie's eyes on her. *Oh yeah, she saw me all right*. "Nope. Gidget's got short legs and I'm just a tiny package. Can you help me up? My knees are scraped right down to the bone."

Grace grabbed Ruby's hands and pulled. The two swayed back and forth like kids on a teeter totter until Rochelle ran to help.

"What're you two doing? You'll hurt yourselves."

The girl's ponytail of red, corkscrew curls draped over Ruby's face and she spat out hair. "Um, I fell down." That was true. She had fallen under the desk. "Grace was just helping me up." Also true.

"Oh, well next time call out for help. At the rate you're going, you'll both end up on the floor."

When the nurse aide had moved away, Ruby said, "I can't wait to try my next hair color. Green is obviously bad luck."

"I'd say you were extraordinarily lucky not to get caught at whatever you were doing."

Ruby shrugged and pursed her lips. "Maybe you're right. The plan went off with only a minor hitch. Now… we wait."

"Don't tell me. I already know too much."

"Okay, I won't, but… you'll know when the fireworks begin."

Ruby toddled up to the staffroom and sidled past in slow motion. Gidget was pouring a cup of coffee from a steel thermos.

Ruby sat in the chair closest to the lounge doors and waited, rubbing her hands with glee.

Thirty minutes later, Bridget emerged from the staff room singing loudly, "I've got a lovely bunch of coconuts," and swigging from her thermos.

"Blast off!" Ruby called out to Melanie who stood near the television, "Hey, Nurse Moth, you wanna see this! Your Kommandant seems to be drunk. Isn't that grounds for expulsion?"

Melanie's eyes widened. "Where?"

Ruby pointed.

The facility manager was in the corridor, dancing a jig to music only she could hear.

Melanie clapped a hand over her mouth. "Nurse Piggott, are you drunk? You know that's a violation of your contract."

The full-bodied woman stomped and hollered, "Yee-haw!" while her multiple rolls bounced in rhythm.

"Nurse Piggott. Did you hear me? I'm going to contact the trustees."

Bridget took another swig and brown liquid dribbled from her mouth. "Go ahead and fire me. I hate my job. This is the best coffee I've ever had."

Melanie squared her sights on Ruby. "Did you do this?"

Ruby placed a hand over her heart and blinked. "Me? How could *I* make her drunk?"

"Mrs. Smith, you're a handful."

"Thank you. So I've been told. Apparently I bring out the worst in people."

An hour later, Melanie appeared in Ruby's room. "She's gone and she's not coming back."

Ruby licked her lips, fear thickening her tongue. "Are you going to send me to Twin Oaks?"

Melanie crossed her arms and leaned against the wall. "That depends."

"On what?"

"How rude you are to me."

Ruby pondered on that. "Just think how dull Sorrento would be without me. How about a 24-hour truce?"

"Not good enough," Melanie countered. "One week!"

Ruby wrinkled her nose. "A whole week?"

"Yes."

"All at one time?"

"Yes," Melanie said.

"I don't think I can handle that."

Melanie inspected her unpolished nails as she spoke. "I hear the beds at Twin Oaks are more comfortable than ours."

Ruby swallowed hard. She would never like this woman. She was as loopy as a bucket of frogs, but Melanie held the winning hand. She sighed in resignation. "You've got a deal, Nurse Moth." She spat on her hand and held it out. Much to her surprise, Melanie spat on hers and slapped Ruby's hand.

"Done."

Peace reigned on the west wing as Ruby and Melanie dodged each other. On the eighth day, Ruby awoke in eager anticipation. After breakfast with Barney Baldwin, she waited in her room, tapping her fingertips together.

Rochelle barged in. "Come on, let's do this quick. I don't want Melanie to catch me. I like my job."

"Don't worry about her. How's your night school going? I'll miss you when you qualify as a hairdresser."

"I'll miss you, too, and I like practicing on you. Maybe I'll visit and do free touch-ups."

"I'm *touched* that you'll do my touch-ups. But I can pay. No problem. You're a good kid."

Sporting her new look, Ruby found Grace in the lounge. "I've seen you cozying up to that Moth nurse all week. Traitor!"

"I like her. She's got a warm heart," Grace said.

"Houston, we have a problem. I have a reputation to uphold, so I can't be friends with the friend of my enemy. You have to choose."

Grace smiled and nodded. "We had a great adventure together, Ruby. That makes us associates forever, but it wouldn't look right to hang out together. I have a reputation, too. Oh dear. What shall we do?"

Ruby slapped her hands together. "I've got it. Let's meet in your room once a week, eat chocolate and have a giggle."

"Great idea!" Grace tipped her head to one side. "I love the new hair color. You trying it out?"

"Nope." Ruby's smile lit the room. "Orange is the winner. It speaks volumes about my personality before I even open my mouth."

***

BIO: Jianna is the author of the Sorrento series and she is currently working on the Silver Sleuth series. Ruby Smith is one of the characters in the series, and Just Kidding is a prequel staring Ruby. Jianna's books have won two Gold medals and three Honorable Mention medals in the Global Ebook Awards, an Honorable Mention medal in the Readers' Favorite International Book Awards, and they have been short-listed finalists in other contests including the Kindle Best Indie Book Awards, Chanticleer Book Awards and the Writers' Village International Novel Contest. Jianna loves chocolate, supporting the All Blacks rugby team and sliding on snow.

http://jiannahiggins.com/

Long Live the Queen
by S. Joan Popek
Head Judge, CWI Staff & Award Winning Author

"I knew we would find the answer here. It had to be here." Her whispers echoed through the dusty archives as if tiny, hidden imps had picked up her words and rolled them back to her across the dry hardwood floor. "Look, Father Paul." Shannon shoved the heavy, leather bound volume closer to the flashlight he held in an unsteady hand.

Under the small circle of light, he saw a page laden with flowing, ornate script. The thick, black ink had blurred with the years, and the paper had weathered to a dark tan. "It's in Latin," he said. "Something about a ritual sacrifice and... an… innocent. There are some numbers here. A five, I think. And a six." He pointed to a faded line, his finger stark white in the small circle of light. And something about... uh... I'm not sure." He lowered the flashlight leaving the two of them dimly illuminated in the light's reflection off the floor. "I'm sorry. I can't quite make that third line out."

She glanced up at him. "I know it's old and faded, but according to what you just read and what I already know, after the first five sacrifices, an innocent's blood is shed. The sixth one… must be an innocent. Then the ritual will be complete. The witch will gain immortality." Her turquoise eyes seemed to glow like a cat's as she strained to see his face in the dim glow of the flashlight. Lowering her gaze back to the ancient book in her hands, she slowly closed it. "Father? Who is more innocent than a child?"

Father Paul could not summon an answer. He watched her slender shoulders tremble as she clutched the bulky volume to her bosom. The deserted library's archive shelves shrouded the room and seemed to hover over their heads like ancient birds of prey. He moved to her and gently pried her hand from its grip on the book. She seemed so fragile – so willing to grasp at anything that might help in her search.

"Shannon, it's just a legend from an old book. We don't know if that's why the statue was stolen from the church. We don't know for sure that they have your daughter." His words were calm – logical – but the bitter taste of a lie churned his stomach. The thieves had the priceless statue and probably her daughter, but the thought of the two of them going after those vile murderers alone frightened him more than he was willing to admit.

Choking back the bile in his throat, he deliberately sought her eyes and held them with what he hoped was a convincing look. An intangible current ran through him as he laid his hand on her arm in a comforting gesture. He let go quickly and felt a chill that was even more unnerving than the fear of why the holy statue had been stolen. This young woman stirred feelings in him that he hadn't felt since he took his vows – feelings he shouldn't be having now.

Memories of this afternoon, when he had first met Shannon, flashed across his mind. She held a newspaper in her hand and waved it in front of him. It was folded to a story about a stolen statue from a local church. She said a witches' coven stole her child and she believed the theft of the statue and the disappearance of her daughter were connected.

Shannon huddled closer to him in the feeble light, bringing his thoughts back to the present. He caught the scent of her skin--the fragrance of her short blonde hair. *She's fascinating,* he thought. Shocked at his thoughts, he mentally berated himself. *You are a priest. There are some things God will not forgive.* Not looking at her, he stepped back and pretended to look for more books as he calmed his pounding heart.

He knew he should have called the Bishop this afternoon when Shannon first explained why she had come to his office. He had no experience with cults or Satanism, but he had been so sure that his faith could withstand anything. In the bright, afternoon sunshine, he had been sure that if he could find the statue and the missing girl, Bishop Trent would have to notice him. He would no longer be the new, untried priest in the parish.

Now, in the darkness of the deserted library archives, the horrifying truth descended upon him with weighty reality. Satanists were real. The missing child was real. What made him think he could fight such depravity alone? He wondered who he was really trying to impress. The Bishop? Shannon? God? "Foolish pride," he mumbled.

"What, Father? What did you say?"

"Nothing... nothing."

Her slim hand flew to his shoulder, nails digging into the flesh beneath the cloth. "Father, don't try to tell me there isn't something to this legend. Too much fits. The statue. Four missing people. The blood drained from their bodies. Two more still missing. That's six – six people, and one is a child. My child! The legend calls for the blood of six to flow over the virgin, and the last must be an innocent. How much more evidence do you need? Father, she's my baby. My little girl. She's only six years old." Her voice became a strangled sob, then a wailing shriek. "In the name of God, please help me!"

He felt paralyzed by the wave of emotion that washed over him. In the wake of her misery, his heart hammered in his chest, and fear flooded his senses. "I will, Shannon. I will, but we must do this the right way."

Her jaw tightened as she clenched her teeth and hissed, "There is only one way to fight this. I don't care if it's right or wrong. We must stop the ritual before it's too late. We must destroy the queen with her own evil!" Her grip on his shoulder tightened.

The ghosts of her pronouncement rumbled through the archives for what seemed an eternity, then silence fell over the two as heavy and solid as granite. The imperial stacks of ancient books encircling them seemed to lean forward in the shadows. The musty odor from decaying pages suggested forgotten mysteries should lie with their long-dead masters.

His trembling hand covered her pale fingers and loosened the hand on his shoulder. Trying to mask his fear, he spoke gruffly. "We've already violated one law by breaking into the private archives. Now you want to pursue people you think *may* be murderers because they *might* have your daughter? Shannon, we must go to the police. It's their job."

"No police! I told you! Even if they believed us, the queen would know. The witch queen would escape. I'd never see my daughter alive again. No, Father. No Police! That's why we had to wait until the library closed before we came here. If we had applied for permission, *she* would have known."

"But how? How could she know?"

"She knows everything. She has lines of communication that you can't even imagine." Shannon tightened her hold on the book and stiffened her shoulders. Her face bore the mark of determination. "That creature is taking revenge on me through my baby. With or without you, I'm going after her. My daughter is all I live for. She's the only good thing in my life. I've got to try!"

He knew he couldn't stop her, and it was too late to ask the Bishop for help. If he left for help now, Shannon would go alone and he couldn't let that happen. Shannon knew the legends, the rituals, and the only way to stop the sacrifice. Her mother had taught her well.

He cringed inwardly, and his hand unconsciously made the sign of the Cross. He shuddered when he thought of what she must have suffered as a child, raised in a cult that dedicated its children to Satan the day they were born.

He remembered how helpless she had seemed this afternoon. She swore she knew who had stolen the sacred statue and begged for his help. As she told her story, she gave glimpses of the rituals she had witnessed, the blasphemous baptisms, human torture and sacrifices convinced him she was telling the truth. She had cried and said that if her father hadn't stolen her from the cult and placed her in the Sisters of Mercy Convent, she might still be one of them.

She had sat on the edge of the leather visitor's chair as if prepared to flee any moment. Her long fingers nervously caressed its worn arm, then found their way to her pouting lips where they rested a moment as she nibbled at them with small, white teeth. Tears traced sharp lines down her pale cheeks as she explained her renounce of the coven. Now her mother, the strongest witch in the coven and a personal favorite of the High Warlock, was punishing her by stealing her child. Shannon vowed to fight with any weapons she had.

Father Paul believed her, though he feared for her life and soul. *God, help us both*, he prayed silently as he crossed himself again, then whispered aloud, "All right. You win. Let's go." Not knowing why, he added, "And bring the book with you."

A murky fog wrapped itself around them when they entered the dark alley outside the library building. The midnight moon hid behind angry, black clouds. Shannon reached for his hand and squeezed it like a child needing reassurance. Reflexively, his hand tightened around hers.

A few minutes later, they stood at the entrance to the Cathedral. Its portals loomed before them, the doorway almost invisible as it crouched amid ancient, intricately carved stone. Two giant gargoyles standing guard on each side grinned menacingly while casting spiked shadows across the seemingly endless stairway leading to the altar.

"I wonder why they're here. This is a house of God. A place of worship. Why would they come here to worship the devil?" Father Paul already guessed the answer, but hoped he was wrong. The thought of such atrocities being conducted in his church sent cold fingers slithering across his heart.

"What better place to defile God than in his own house?" she said. "Besides, this cathedral has a history." Her voice was filled with such venom that Paul spun to face her.

"History?"

"Witches have conducted their most depraved ceremonies in the caves beneath this church since the eighteenth century. Only the highest and most profane can come here... or even know about it."

"How do you know? Have you been here

before?"

"Twice." Her face held poisonous hatred. Pain twisted her soft lips into thin, white lines weighted with malevolence. "This is where I was baptized into the coven. They do it with blood instead of water. Want to see the scars?" Her eyes narrowed into scalding pellets as she began to lift her blouse.

"NO! No… I… I had no idea." His constricted throat would let no more words pass his lips. He, a priest of God, stood in the dark portal staring at her young face, and he could think of no comforting words from God or anyone else. Her misery overwhelmed his senses. He wanted to run, but her agony froze him into immobility.

Her eyes became warm again. Her voice softened. "I'm sorry Father. Sometimes the memories are… very… please forgive me."

"There is nothing to forgive, my child." His body thawed, and his reserve faith strengthened. He fought down the anger and fear the scene awakened in him. Taking her hand, he turned toward the stairway. "Where do we go from here?"

She led him in silence as they climbed to the top of the stairs.

"Behind the altar," she whispered. "There's a trap door. Twist the left arm of the Christ figure all the way back."

He approached the Christ figure slowly. Twisting an arm would be like desecration. What if the arm broke off? A one-armed Christ would be hard to explain and harder to forget. Deliberately avoiding the figure's accusing eyes, he twisted the arm.

The grinding sound of stone against stone startled him as a hidden door creaked open. The screech thundered loud enough to awaken even the ancient dead in the chapel's cemetery. When the scream of the stones halted, a wailing chant drifted up through the opening. His faith faltered. *I've got to get Bishop Trent. We can't do this alone,* he thought.

Trembling, he turned to grab Shannon and flee from this hellish place, but she bulldozed past him, running down the black, granite steps leading toward the incantations.

"Shannon! Wait! Don't!" He surged after her, though his mind screamed in protest. Heart pounding, lungs fighting for air, mindlessly… he followed the desperate girl down the dark, shadowed passageway.

You can't let her face them alone. You're a priest. Remember your vows! His priestly conscience fought the traitorous, frightened body that only wanted to turn and run back up the stairs.

Flickering torch light glowed ahead. Shannon slowed. Her finger touched her lips, motioning him to be quiet.

Shallow breaths robbed him of oxygen. He leaned heavily against the cool, stone walls.

"Shhh. She's here. I feel her. She knows we're here."

"Your daughter?"

"No. The witch. My beloved mother!" she sneered. "They're coming for us."

Black-robed figures seemed to fade into reality out of thin air. They were surrounded. The priest grabbed her hand and tried to run, but hands that were not hands, more like claws, raked into his arms. Where they touched him, a burning itch began and coursed down his side in sharp, fiery streaks. Black hoods obscured their faces, but he felt with a rising fear that they had no eyes, perhaps not even faces!

A warm dampness pervaded the air. Dusky

wisps of smoke trailed the heavy torches they carried. He sucked in the clammy air and felt its suffocating wetness fill his lungs. He squinted to see beyond the smoke, but it burned his eyes until they filled with tears. It was like trying to see through murky water. The black robes propelled them toward a vast chamber peopled by hundreds of shadowy figures who seemed to waver, floating just beyond Father Paul's vision. When he turned to look at them, they shifted and were once again just out of sight. The chanting ceased abruptly. Silence shrouded the room.

The black robes halted.

Their captors parted.

A large stone altar surrounded by flaming torches came into view.

Father Paul's vision cleared. His heart plunged to his guts.

The stolen, Sacred Virgin statue stood on the floor beneath the altar in a pool of blood. A crimson stain flowed lazily around her golden crown and rained across her sculpted face like ruby tears. The statue's bowed head seemed to be pointing at a crumpled, large doll covered with fresh blood lying on the floor beside it.

Dear God, it's not a doll! Paul's mind refused to accept what he saw… a man, probably young, with a gaping hole where the heart should have been.

Tearing his eyes from the horrifying scene, he raised his head to see a small, blond figure lying atop the altar, her eyes fixed on the glinting dagger held above her.

There stood the most exquisite naked woman. Voluptuous. Menacing. Beguiling. Intriguing. Captivating. Both arms raised, she held a dagger in one hand, and blood ran down her other arm in rivulets as the pulsating, fleshy mass in her hand oozed red, viscous fluid.

In the silence, Father Paul heard the rhythmic beat of the dead man's heart… plop… plop… plop… echoing across the cavern as the crimson stream dripped ran down the woman's nude body and onto the stone floor.

When she turned her midnight eyes to him, he was riveted to the spot. She invaded his mind – his flesh. He fought as his body slumped into a gesture of worship on the cold stone. With head bowed and knees bent, demons cackled from every corner. He struggled to regain his feet. They were as heavy as granite.

"Stupid priest," the woman said as she spat. "Did you really think you could defeat me? Worship me, you fool!"

Abundant ebony hair snaked around her shoulders, caressed her hips and slithered between her thighs as though it were alive. For a moment, she stood seducing him, mocking him, her cruel eyes glazed.

A fissure of light formed next to her and a massive male creature appeared. Smooth, black membranes hugged his lean body, writhing with an enticing pulsation, completely independent of the frame it caressed. The man's gaunt, pale face wore a look of absolute victory. His sooty eyes flashed flame as sneering lips stretched into a grin. A black hole opened where his mouth should have been, and out of the hole came a fiendish howl that echoed across the cavern.

"Father! Don't look at him!" Shannon said. "Father – my daughter – my Cassandra – look! Oh, no!" Now in a total panic, eyes wild, full understanding hit her. "I thought they used her to bring me, but they wanted *her*! They're going to *immortalize* her!"

Shannon's outcry broke the spell the two figures on the altar had over the priest. Tremors shook him as, with a reluctance he found repulsive, he tore his eyes away from the queen witch and focused on the small, scarlet-robed figure lying quietly on the altar.

Power surged through his body, pulling him from his forced kneeling position. He fought, to no avail, as he lunged at the queen. Her fiery eyes flashed lightning into his brain and hurled him onto the altar. His flesh crawled with agony as his hands fumbled for the child beneath him. He screamed in both defiance and fear as his arms encircled the child, picked her up and thrust her small body toward Shannon. "Catch her!" he shrieked.

Another bolt of lightning flashed. His head ground into the stone floor. Enraged screams issued from somewhere behind him – and then the pitch black swallowed him.

As cognizance thrashed with the vail that surrounded him, he became dimly aware of Shannon standing over him. Her slim figure held the child behind her with one hand and the ancient, leather book in front of her like a shield with the other.

Flames blazed from her eyes as she stared at the queen. Lightning flashed past him – around him – then through him. Spasms of agony racked his body into jelly as the sepulchral voice of the queen exploded.

"Turn on me, will you, Shannon? Weakling! You can't stop me with your flimsy powers. I am the queen! And your daughter is my princess. She will take your place as my companion throughout eternity."

Father Paul prayed, and the pain became bearable. Strength surged through his limp body and thoughts cleared. He and Shannon were alone with the child and the witch queen now.

Shannon still faced the fiend on the dais, but the child was weakening. Shannon's eyes betrayed her fear as she glanced down at him, then jerked her head up quickly to meet the queen's onslaught. A slashing light flashed through one side of her body and out the other. She screamed and then whispered, "Father, can you move? I… I can't hold Cassandra much longer!" Her face drained as she sent one last surge of lightning to the queen before she collapsed onto the floor.

The naked woman pitched back and lost her footing on the blood-slick stone. Ebony hair cascaded around her like a black, velvet cape. Regaining her balance, she filled her lungs with a shuddering breath, pulled up slowly, and stretched menacing arms toward Shannon.

Instinctively, Paul knew it was the death blow. "NO!" Father Paul lunged at the Queen and clutched her throat. He cried – he screamed – but he did not – he could not – let go. "Help me, God. Strengthen me," he shrieked in prayer. Over his shoulder he shouted, "Run Shannon! Take Cassandra! RUN!"

"Fool!" The queen clutched his face with strong fingers and covered his mouth with hers. Her breath seared his insides, and still he held her throat in the death grip.

She pulled her mouth from his, and clutched the sides of his head and squeezed like a vise.

He screamed as the pressure increased, and he screeched at the top of his lungs when his skull cracked, but he continued to bury his thumbs in her throat.

Her black eyes captured his. "Pray… to your… God," she croaked. "He will not… help you. You… have sinned. Your lust has denied… your priesthood. You are… a prisoner of Satan. *My…* prisoner."

"Forgive me, God, for I have sinned!" His fingers tightened around her neck as he yelled. "Forgive me… God… for… I… have sinned!" Her blood pounded past his unrelenting fingers, down them… into him. "Forgive me, God, for I have sinned!" His heart picked up the beat of hers – *thunder-thud-thunder-thud.* The beat slowed – *thrush-thrush.*

"For… give… me… Lor… And still his hands gripped.

Fear flared in the queen's eyes. Her flesh melted into his. Twisting and turning, her body swirled into the air with his, slamming him against the jagged edges of the cave wall, but he held on. Smashing him against the icy floor, but he held on.

Every muscle in his body cried for mercy. Still he held onto her throbbing neck.

She was invading him now… smothering him. Her face became the man's, but with no mouth.

A hole opened in his face. "Forgive me, God, for I have sinned," the words whispered on the air. He squeezed tighter. Her face became Shannon's. He forced his eyes shut against the face he knew was not real – and still he held on. "Forgive me… God… for I have… sinned!"

Her neck cracked within his hands--bone met flesh--her blood joined his as it cascaded through his fingers—but still he held on.

"JOIN… ME… IN HELL… PRIEST!" She said as she spat a final flash of venomous flame into his holy face, shrieked, and pulled them both aloft as they struggled.

Her neck snapped, and the pair plummeted down... her lifeless body crumpling onto the bloody, sacrificial altar. Hurricane-like winds thrust him across the room and smashed his body against the unforgiving cavern wall. He felt his bones pulverize--organs became pulp—and he slithered down the wall to rest on the cold, wet floor.

I feel no pain, he thought with surprise. *There should be pain.* He closed his eyes gratefully.

"Father Paul! Father, please don't die. Father?" Shannon's pleading voice opened his eyes.

"You... are beautiful," he breathed in a coughing whisper. "Take... Cassandra... go."

"I can't leave you, Father."

"You... must."

"Father, you saved her life. I can't..." Her tears fell on his forehead as she gently stroked his cheek.

Her hand felt cool. With a weak gasp, he sighed, "Not me... Shannon... don't... follow me... follow... God."

A child knelt beside the priest and gazed into his hazy eyes. A golden halo of hair shimmered around her delicate, innocent face.

It's Shannon's daughter, Cassandra... how pretty she is. How like an angel, he thought. *It was worth it.*

Cassandra bent over him. Soft lips touched his, and the girl whispered in his ear. "Sleep well, priest. And thank you. Now that the queen is dead, *I* am the queen. Long live the queen!" As she raised her head, her perfect face wore a sad smile that masked her mocking, turquoise eyes. She turned to take Shannon's hand and in a soft, child's voice said, "Come, Mother. We must go."

Horror froze his heart. He tried to scream--to warn Shannon. He knew she wouldn't allow herself to believe anything evil of her daughter until it was too late. The priest's eyes fluttered with the greatest of effort. His mouth opened and Shannon put her ear to his mouth as he tried to speak, but no sound came from his broken body.

His eyes clouded over. Darkness gathered. He felt, with a sense of reverence, the final flutter of his heart as the immortal child led her mother toward the yawning blackness of the cavern tunnel.

***

BIO: S. Joan Popek was owner and editor of Millennium Science Fiction & Fantasy Magazine and The Roswell Literary Review. She also wrote a monthly column called Ask Dr. WEB-Write for Millennium. She has been published in over 250 fiction, nonfiction and poetry works in various magazines. Her books, The Administrator, Sound The Ram's Horn, and Fairy Tales With A Freudian Flair are available from Amazon. The Administrator won the 2000 EPPIE Award, and her nonfiction book, Jumpstart Your Career With Electronic Publishing, was a 2002 EPPIE Finalist.

http://www.sjoanpopek.com/

The Angel of Death
by L. Edward Carroll
Contest Judge & CWI Staff

Some people don't believe it, but I met the Angel of Death. It was December 21, 1944, and World War II was on everyone's mind. My seventh birthday was just eight days away. I didn't know it at the time, but apparently, everyone else in the family knew I had only a few months to live.

My father and two uncles were away at war. Mother worked as a welder in some sort of war assembly plant all night, and she slept all day. Grandmother Crenshaw took me and my cousins, a total of six, to live with her in the big yellow Victorian house that had a wrap-around porch.

School was out for the Christmas holiday, and all the kids were home. Every morning after breakfast, I would watch the other kids laughing, pushing, and shoving to be the first to play with the neighborhood kids.

Despite the warnings from Grandmother Crenshaw *not* to, they invariably let the door slam behind them so you can imagine what a racket that was all day. I had been too ill to join in for the past few months, so I went into the parlor room – a room strictly reserved for special occasions – but now open to only me because of my health.

On the 21st of each December, Grandmother Crenshaw decorated the parlor for the Christmas season. I have still never seen a Christmas tree so beautifully prepared. When I asked if I could help, she chuckled and said, "No, sweetie, I don't want any help. It has to be done just so, and some of these ornaments have been in the family for over a hundred years and I'm afraid they might get broken."

Strings of popcorn, paper chains made by us kids, and multi-colored lights decorated the trees. We called the lights 'glass candles' and they bubbled constantly, each one perfectly placed for maximum effect. I sat for hours breathing in the heady aroma of that perfectly decorated blue spruce, eating every minute.

"Ah! There you are," Grandma said.

I turned and there she stood, a warm, heavy-set woman with beautiful silver hair. She put her arms around me and gently squeezed. I remember the distinct odor of nutmeg and cinnamon. Always cheerful, and with those rosy cheeks, she reminded me of Mrs. Santa Claus.

"Are you alright?" she said. "Are you hungry, sweetie?"

I shook my head. "Grandmother, I love your tree. It's so beautiful."

"Thank you, honey. Come, sit." She motioned to her special wing-backed chair, the arms and headrest covered with her hand-made lace doilies. "I have something to tell you. We're going to have a prayer meeting for you and Reverend Strawbridge will be here."

I listened as she described the healing circle and she talked about God and other such stuff. Much of what she was saying is a blur now, but I understood there would be a healing prayer circle the next morning. At the time, I thought it was a lot of fuss over nothing, but then, I didn't know I was dying.

After our talk… her talk… she gave a quick nod, patted my little pointed head and bustled back to her kitchen. That old Victorian house carried wafts of fried chicken and apple and mincemeat pies in every crack and crevice.

I could hear Grandma splitting small kindling with a butcher knife in preparation for supper. I remember the wood-burning stove/oven and how Princess, Grandmother's cat, slept under it. It puzzled me how she knew exactly what size kindling and precisely how much to place under each burner. How she could perfectly control the heat with the damper in the stovepipe and kindling, I'll never know. Yes, electric stoves were available, but she preferred the antique wood-burning stove.

Supper was always fit for the King of England and other such dignitaries. However, having no appetite, I stayed in the parlor and watched the snow fall. I could see the reflection in the big bay window next to that magical, aromatic blue spruce Christmas tree.

I vaguely remember someone carrying me upstairs to my bedroom. Later, I awoke to the sound of people talking downstairs and since my room had a floor grate that allowed heat to rise from the coal stove, I laid on the floor, opened the slats all the way, and heard everything that was going on below.

The adults, under the supervision of Grandma Crenshaw, dragged the heavy round dining table from the center to one corner of the room. It went easily enough because the eagle claws carved into the wooden legs held large green glass balls that rolled with a little rumble.

Next, they moved all the chairs and knickknack tables to the living room, and left one armless chair smack dab in the middle of the dining room. How curious.

When everyone left, I could hear Grandmother and Grandfather talking.

"I don't know why you fuss over that boy so much. What's gonna happen is gonna happen anyway."

"Oh, hush your mouth, you old goat. Go finish your beer and go to bed."

Puzzled, I returned to my bed, and before I could digest what that was all about, fell asleep.

The next morning, after breakfast, the family and a host of long-lost relatives gathered in the large dining room and Grandmother escorted me to the chair in the middle of the room. So there I sat, surrounded by Mother, aunts, Grandmother, and Grandfather and a lot of strangers standing in a circle around me. There was a strange absence of children, which made me a bit uncomfortable, and before they even started, Grandfather excused himself and went outside. I knew where he was going. There was a tavern one block down the street. Everyone knew each other down there, and Grandfather was perhaps the most known of all.

Reverend Strawbridge, a tall, lanky bald man wearing a frightful scowl on his saggy old face, joined me in the middle of the circle. When he tried to place his hand on my head, I ducked, but Grandmother said, "It's alright, Samuel. Let the Reverend place his hand on your head. Everything's going to be fine."

I sat still, but rolled my eyes up. The Reverend's other hand held a raggedy Bible. He told everybody to join hands and he began praying. I didn't comprehend most of what he was saying as he droned on and on. I was looking at the gnarled hand holding the Bible. His fingernails were yellow and cracked, and his knuckles looked like marbles under his liver-spotted skin. I'll bet I was the only one to notice that. And then I heard a dog barking.

After what seemed like an eternity of more prayers, they sang hymns, and Grandma said I could get some rest. A little while later, they moved the chairs and the big round dining table back to the middle of the room, threw a white tablecloth over it, and set food out for everyone.

Suddenly, all the missing kids piled in and took their seat at the children's table in the kitchen. Reverend Strawbridge ate his weight in potato salad and cold fried chicken and Grandma Crenshaw gave him a whole mincemeat pie to take home.

I clearly remember the great heap of presents under the blue spruce and how excited I was. I don't remember what any of the presents were, but I was very disappointed that I only got one of them. My birthday followed a few days later, but that did little or nothing to salve my wounds.

On the night before my birthday, I got out of bed and went downstairs to relieve myself. On the way back, the steep, narrow stairway was, as Grandmother Crenshaw would say, "as dark as the inside of a black cat." Downright eerie. When I got a little more than halfway, I noticed a bright pinpoint of light floating at the top of the stairs. There was no lamp up there. Scared as I was, I stared until it suddenly disappeared.

I almost ran to bed, jumped in and pulled the covers up to my chin, and the same light showed up at the foot of my bed. My eyes must have bugged as it went from a pinpoint to a point where its light flooded the room. Almost blind and paralyzed with fear, I tried to scream, but I couldn't move or even breathe, let alone make a sound. My heart beat so hard that I thought it would break my chest, and then… as suddenly as it appeared… it was gone. I sucked in a big gulp of air and forcibly held in a scream. I covered my head and shivered until dawn. It was my birthday, and I was anxious to get downstairs and open my presents.

My appetite was much improved and brought smiles to Grandmother Crenshaw. Food never tasted so good. The kids, amazed, looked at each other, shrugged, and bolted for the mudroom to dress for snowball fights and sledding in the front yard.

"Hold on," Grandmother said. "Every one of you get back here. This is Sammy's birthday and you are going to watch him open his presents."

A lot of groans and sighing met the ceiling, but they all sat at the table while I opened them. I gloated over the fact that I had presents and no one else did, but as soon as I opened the last one, the kids scrambled for the mudroom to dress for outdoors.

"Grandmother, can I go out and play today?" I said.

"Not yet, sweetie."

"When Grandmother? I feel fine. Honest, I really feel fine."

She looked at me, smiled, and said, "Maybe in a few weeks."

The wait was eternal and I begged every day. Finally, two weeks later, she agreed. For the first time in almost six months, I joined my cousins outside. Still weak from a mostly bedridden lifestyle, I enjoyed the biting cold air and the squeaking sound the snow made when I walked on it. I could smell wood burning in the fireplaces along our street and a new appreciation of life blossomed. Everything was fresh and sweet. Awesome! Wonderful! Like a magical wonderland.

"Hey, Sammy," Uncle Brian shouted. "You

want another ride up the street?"

I jumped on the sled. "You bet!"

It's been many years, and since that bizarre encounter with the light, I have enjoyed good health. It was much later that I learned the doctors could not identify my illness. The diagnosis was a blood disorder of unknown origin. They could not account for the draining strength any more than the symptoms suddenly disappearing.

Years later, when Grandmother Crenshaw was in an assisted-living home, I told her my secret. "Grandmother, I never told you or anyone else about the strange light I saw that night after the prayer circle in 1944."

"What do mean? What light? Speak up, boy, I can barely hear you."

"Well," I said, leaning closer, "it was a small light at first, and then it grew into a huge bright light. I was in bed and I was scared stiff. I couldn't even scream for help. I thought I was going to die."

"Well, we didn't want you to know that you were…"

"Yeah, I know, but here's the thing – the next day, I felt better than I have ever felt and I've never been sick since. I've been wondering…"

Grandmother interrupted. "I've always known you were cured because of the prayer circle with Reverend Strawbridge."

"Yes, but I still wonder what that strange light was."

"I wish you had told me about this back then, but I can tell you what I think. I think it was the Angel of Death who came to give you a pass."

That conversation occurred just days before she passed over to the Promised Land. I must admit, I think she was right, and I often wonder if she saw the same light.

***

BIO: L. Edward Carroll is a graduate of Long Ridge Writers Group, The Institute of Children's Literature, and is a former writing tutor at A-1 Writing Academy. He also has a background as a Computer Systems Analyst, has an Economics major, and is a former entrepreneur. Born and raised in Greenfield, Massachusetts, this ex-Marine drill sergeant now devotes himself to drilling fledgling writers at Creative Writing Institute.

The Forest Painter
by Diane Mae Robinson
Contest Judge, CWI Staff
& Award Winning Children's Author

Deep in the woods of Majestic Forest, the song of the Great Bugle was just being delivered from the misty heights of Peak Mountain. The changing of the seasons had arrived. Leaf-gathering sprites, cloud-shaping elves, and all the wind weavers recognized the summons and were slowly emerging from their sleepy hollows. Soon, every creature of autumn's magic would be hustling about, eager to perform their duties of the season.

All except one.

Aura circled the eldest Poplars, eyeing the trees suspiciously as they swayed and seemed to clap their faded green hands in anticipation. She tugged the paintbrush from the tangles of her hair and threw it to the ground. "The forest is too big! I don't know how to do this!"

"But, my lady, you must do it. You are the forest painter now," the pixie, Kepa, spoke softly as she fluttered down to perch on Aura's shoulder. "And by the laws of Majestic Forest, the leaves must breathe with autumn beauty before the frost queen arrives, or she will claim the forest white forever. Look there— the glitters and sparkles and velvet colors. I have them all ready."

Aura flapped her wings hard, sending Kepa tumbling through the air. "My grandmother was the master painter, not me! Then, without warning, she was called upon to paint the heavens where my parents dwell forever. I never learned the art . . . I thought we would have more time together."

Kepa zipped back. "My lady, then might you ask Boreal for help? He was your grandmother's friend, and the Star Master is the greatest of artists. The elves say he taught them wonderful new images for their cloud art and surely—"

"No, not Boreal! He will try to steal the golden paintbrush from me just as I saw him steal it from my grandmother once. If he was a friend, explain how that happened! How could Boreal be trusted ever again?"

Kepa placed the golden paintbrush in Aura's palm. "Then you must try by yourself. But sometimes it is worth knowing that you must see with your heart, not only your eyes."

Aura stood in silence for some time. "Get the glitter paint ready," she ordered. "At least, my eyes tell me I have work to do."

Throughout the day, Kepa mixed and toned the paint while Aura hovered above the trees, hurling thick splatters of glitter onto the leaves. "My lady, the sun will soon sleep beyond Peak Mountain, and I fear you have not accomplished as much as need be done."

"I still have time." Aura glanced at the deep hues of pink and purple as dusk settled on the horizon, creating a cape around Peak Mountain. She inhaled a deep breath of the crisp fall air. "Prepare the sparkles, Kepa."

Aura slapped the brush into the new color and flew with spins and dives, splashing globs of sparkles over the wet glitter.

Kepa's shriek pierced the air before she called out, "I'm sure the frost queen's fingers have, just now, tickled my spine. She is nearer than the north wind has told. Will you not reconsider? I am sure Boreal would help."

"No. I can do it alone!" Aura snapped, wiping her forehead. But she too had felt the icy breath on the back of her neck, and it taunted her with whispers of its claim to the forest. "Look, the moonlight has come on now. We can work throughout the night. Hurry yourself, Kepa. Finish with the velvet color."

Aura grabbed a bucket of the velvet paint and, flying in a zigzag pattern, tilted the bucket enough to let the paint spill out in a steady stream. She returned for the second bucket just as clouds started dancing across the moon. The shadows made it difficult for her to tell where she had left off. An idea sprung to her. In one swift motion, she heaved up the full bucket and flung the color into the darkness.

Tingles of excitement came over her as she caught glimpses of the velvet curtain slithering over the leaves and down the tree trunks. "See, Kepa, I'm nearly done and it is not even nearing the dawn."

"True, my lady," the pixie whispered, "but what of the soul of autumn?"

Aura fluttered down to the ground and wrapped her wings tightly around her body. She shivered as she listened to the "thup, thup, thup" of the paint dripping off the leaves like tears. "Your words ring true," Aura finally decided. "My grandmother's pride is not here. Even the song of the loon is sadder than usual as if he, too, weeps for this autumn." Aura stood up tall. "Call for the Star Master, Kepa. Majestic Forest must not be lost to the frost queen's icy touch!"

Guided by a wind weaver, Kepa soared off on the wings of the wind, soon to return with Boreal to the forest.

"Why, Aura," came a thundering voice from above, "what artist has created autumn this year?" He pushed back the hood of his cloak, revealing his wrinkled face, and his long hair and beard that fell in tangled knots.

Aura clenched her fists. "Boreal, I need help. I fear the frost queen's arrival by this moondown. My heart is willing to forgive you if you will help me save the autumn."

"Forgive me?" Boreal's laughter sent the clouds scattering. "My dear child, I have done you no wrong. My life is in the night sky, creating images of heroes and beasts in the stars and painting the faces of the moon that forever watch over Majestic Forest."

"Then why did you steal the golden paintbrush from my grandmother?" Aura demanded. "I recognized your cloaked figure when you took it from the edge of the river one night."

Boreal smiled and gently touched her wing.

Aura felt energy like a surge of warm tingles rush through her.

"I was only returning the brush to a forgetful old lady," Boreal assured her. "You can trust in me, as well as you should learn to trust in yourself."

Aura stared into the Star Master's ancient face. She noticed how his green eyes twinkled with the same kindness as her grandmother's. He suddenly seemed very wise. "Boreal, will you show me? We haven't much time."

"To be a great artist, you must create with passion," Boreal instructed eagerly. He clasped Aura's hand in his and, with a light, sweeping motion, guided her to gently brush the leaves with a caress of paint. Their tender touch guided the brush to swirl and twirl like a conductor's baton directing the autumn song. The tree limbs seemed to recognize the gesture and bowed down, allowing the leaves to reach out to them.

She practiced the technique on her own, growing more confident in the movements of her hand swaying in a deliberate and delicate dance with the brush and the paint. Before long, she was gliding gracefully, as if to some unheard music, spreading ribbons of billowing velvet and glitter throughout the forest.

An unexpected rage of icy balls plummeted from the sky.

Aura fumbled the brush, nearly losing it to the river below. Gripping the brush tighter, she frantically beat her wings against the stinging balls and shot up over the treetops. "Boreal, Kepa, I must finish the canopy," she called down to them. "Get the sparkles to me, spread them high and wide. Please hurry!"

Kepa hastily stirred the sparkles to bubble up in the last buckets of paint and placed them inside Boreal's cloak.

With a swift and precise sweep of his arm, Boreal raised his cloak to cover all the forest and the sky as he flung the sparkles up toward Aura.

Aura beat her wings with such force that they ached. Even as the air chilled and frost bites nipped at her, sweat beads formed on her brows as she fretted over how to catch all the sparkles before they fell back to the ground. Steadying her breathing, she concentrated harder on her task. Time slowed: the icy balls now fluttered down like harmless snowflakes; the sparkles just hovered in the air as if waiting for her to catch them. She felt time and all of nature becoming one with her in the urgency to claim the autumn.

She gasped when she realized that this power, this magic of thought, was within herself -- she just had to believe. She spread her wings and willingly fell into the waltzing dance of the wind. The mystical rhythm of her flight allowed her to soar with masterful elegance and timeless speed, to precisely zip between every icy ball to gather the sparkles, and to offer each leaf its sparkle crown.

At the exact moment that Aura's paintbrush kissed the last leaf, Boreal's cloak fell back, taking the melting ice balls away in its folds. A trail of fading light followed behind the moon, as if it had just swung back into its place to smile upon the forest again. In the shimmer of moonlight, autumn's masterpiece twinkled like a stash of jewels.

Kepa cheered. Boreal laughed and nodded. The sprites, elves and wind weavers gathered around and broke into applause.

Aura sent out the finale of her thoughts for this autumn -- the remnants of glitter and sparkles and velvet colors swirled into a whirlwind that launched upward, exploding into a light show that danced across the night sky. And just for a breath, as a tear of pride dropped from her eye, the forest painter saw her grandmother's image smiling down at her from the heavens.

***

BIO: Diane Mae Robinson is a multi-award winning children's author and teaches *Writing for Children* at Creative Writing Institute. Diane is also an artist, art teacher, and a freelance children's book editor.

Her children's book series, The Pen Pieyu Adventures, has won ten international book awards and one prestigious provincial award since 2012. The author's newest book, The Dragon Grammar Book, (an easy-to-understand grammar book for middle grades through adults) is due to release in early 2017.

http://www.dragonsbook.com

The Shoebox
by Emily-Jane Hills Orford
Contest Judge and CWI Staff

I placed the shoebox on my desk, pleased that mine at least marginally resembled the shoeboxes that sat on other desks, and pleased that I even had a shoebox. We had just moved to London from Hamilton, Ontario. All empty boxes had long been discarded. It was not a top priority in the keepsake department.

My shoebox had held Barbie doll clothes and thus maintained some value to allow it to be packed and moved along with my dolls and other toys. I had fond memories of the shoes that had been purchased in the very same box... black, patent leather that glistened after a good polish, with hard soles that gave a good clatter on a hardwood floor. They were dress-up shoes, only to be worn with my good clothes, my Sunday best clothes, and only if they fit, which, sadly, they no longer did.

Mrs. Smithers, my fourth-grade teacher, marched to the front of the class and instructed us to take our seats. She handed out sheets of red construction paper, paper lace doilies, scissors and glue.

"Draw your hearts with pencil before you start cutting them out," she said. "I'll come around and cut out the hole in the top, then we'll seal them shut and cover the boxes with your Valentine decorations."

We were making our very own Valentine mailboxes. I couldn't think of a better way to spend the last part of the afternoon than doing crafts. Making a mailbox sounded like so much fun. It would be a real keepsake.

I wondered if I would receive any Valentines. Mom had already put me to work making Valentine cards for all my classmates.

"It's only fair that you give one card to each person in the class," she insisted when I grumbled about giving Valentines to the boys, especially the bullies. Would all the other Mom's insist their children do the same?

Mrs. Smithson made her way around the classroom, cutting holes carefully into the box tops. She stopped by my desk a little longer than the others. "Those are lovely hearts," she said with a big smile.

"Are we going to have a competition for the prettiest Valentine mailbox?" one of the other students asked.

"Well, I don't know," she answered.

"Please," several of the girls echoed in unison.

"But that wouldn't be fair," Mrs. Smithson said. "All of your boxes are starting to look very nice, very attractive. I couldn't possibly choose which one was the prettiest."

Some of the girls muttered under their breaths that their boxes were by far the prettiest. I didn't mind. I knew that for me, my box would always be the best and that was all that mattered.

We finished our Valentine mailboxes and tidied our desks just as the bell rang for dismissal. "Now don't forget to bring your Valentines tomorrow," Mrs. Smithson reminded us as we bundled up to venture out into the cold.

Our Valentine mailboxes were left on our desks overnight. They remained on our desks all through the next day, Valentine's Day. After lunch, the teacher allowed us to hand out our Valentines. It was so much fun walking around the classroom and placing a Valentine card in every mailbox. It was like being a mailman for real. Only it wasn't.

After we were seated again, the last recess bell rang and we were quickly ushered outside. Before following the others to the cloakroom at the back of the portable classroom, I peeked into the opening slot at the top of my box. There wasn't much to see. Only two Valentines lay at the bottom of the box. I was heartbroken. I guess my Mom was the only one who believed in being fair to everyone else.

The class bullies seemed to be aware of my sad state. All through recess, they teased me about my empty Valentine mailbox. I was so glad when the bell finally rang to let us back inside. We shed out coats and boots and resumed our seats. The teacher had set a Valentine cupcake on each of our desks.

"You may look at your Valentines now," she said.

All around me, my classmates were ripping open their boxes and dumping the contents on the desk to sort through. I took a bite of my cupcake and tried to pretend that I was more interested in the cupcake than my Valentine mailbox.

"Aren't you going to look inside?" the teacher said, coming up beside me. "It does look rather full."

I didn't believe her. I had seen the contents of my box before going to recess. "Go on and have a look," she said.

I pulled the box towards me and peaked inside. The teacher was right. It was full of Valentines. "Wow!" I gasped. I carefully unwrapped my box, not wanting to destroy my artwork and dumped the Valentines onto my desk.

"How come you have more Valentines than I

do?" Janice, the class favorite said.

"Yeah!" one of the bullies said. "Explain how that happened. I certainly didn't give you a Valentine."

"Neither did I," Janice said.

I just shrugged my shoulders and opened the top Valentine on the pile. "It's from Jane," I announced.

"Who?" several voices asked.

"Jane," I said. "She's my best friend at my old school." I smiled as I sorted through the rest of the Valentines. They were all from my former classmates. They hadn't forgotten me.

Once I was finished, I looked up at Mrs. Smithson. "Thank you," I said, realizing that she and my mother must have worked together to be sure I had lots of Valentines. Mom must have sent Mrs. Smithson the package of Valentines from my old school so that Mrs. Smithson could stuff them in my Valentine mailbox during the last recess. It was a good feeling to have friends, even if they were in another city and another school.

***

BIO: Emily-Jane Hills Orford has pursued her passion for writing stories about the 'real' people in her life. Her stories have appeared in History Magazine, Canadian Stories Magazine, and Western People. She has published several fiction and creative nonfiction books. Her award-winning novel, *F-Stop: A Life in Pictures* (Baico 2011), is a story about her mother.

http://emilyjanebooks.ca

Tumbling Into Love
by Terri Osburn
Amazon & Wall Street Journal Best Selling Author

This was a deep pile of doo-doo I'd gotten myself
into. Of course the steps were slippery. It was twelve
flipping degrees outside and the world looked like a
winter wonderland. But I'd bought these new boots
expressly for the promise they'd made – traction, even
on ice.

Traction my possibly broken big toe.

I glanced around and found nothing but swirling
snow dancing in the harsh beams of the apartment
complex flood lights. A fine mess indeed. How hard
would it have been to slip my cell phone into my
pocket before leaving the apartment? But then, I'd
only been taking out the garbage. A seemingly non-
dangerous task.

"Help!" I called, praying someone would hear.

My best friend, Katy, who lived across the hall
from me three floors up, would no doubt find this
amusing. "Ducky," she would say, "what have you
done now?"

Why she thought Ducky sounded better than
Daphne, I didn't know. Katy claimed Daphne was old-
fashioned, and often reminded me that she could have
picked a worse nickname, that being Daphy. My
reasonable argument that she could simply call me by
my real name like every other person I knew landed
on deaf ears.

"Help!" I yelled louder. I hadn't been stupid
enough to walk out without my coat, but even wool
had its limits, and the wind whipping through the open

stairwell penetrated my meager outer layer. Not to mention, my toes were growing dangerously numb.

Well, all but the one thumping like a kick drum.

Resigned to my fate, I plucked up the courage to stand up, only to land unceremoniously on my butt the second I put weight on my right foot. So the toe wasn't the only injury. The pain shooting from my ankle sent that message loud and clear.

Tears threatened, but I feared they'd freeze on my cheeks. A quick swipe of my sleeve, followed by several deep breaths until the angry twinge of pain subsided, and I surveyed my circumstances once more.

Five stairs down would get me to the ground. I could make it, slow and steady, clinging to the railing, but once I reached the bottom, the rail would end and any kind of travel would require hopping on one leg. In snow and ice. A daunting scenario, but then again, freezing to death less than thirty feet from my front door was not an acceptable alternative.

Scooting on my butt, I worked my way down, thankful that my coat reached the back of my knees. Once my good foot touched frozen concrete, I hefted my weight to reach an upright position, grabbing the rail as I did so only to be jarred by the sting of cold metal on bare skin. A quick dip into my pockets came up empty.

No gloves. Fabulous.

Leaning against the base of the rail, I took several deep breaths before closing my eyes and sounding the alarm once more.

"Can anyone hear me?"

Like a lifeline from heaven, a voice called back. "Hello? Who's out there?"

My relief didn't last long, as the answering voice

rang all too familiar in my ears.

Why did the only person to hear my plea have to be the man who'd witnessed my most embarrassing moment a mere twenty four hours before? Well, most embarrassing up until this one.

I'd made the mistake the night before of letting Katy mix my drinks at Wilson Sullivan's holiday party. Wilson lived in building four, which was across the commons from our building six. My spontaneous debauchery of the previous night had resulted in my not only depantsing myself and twirling my jeans above my head, breaking Wilson's prized Frankfurt beer stein and nearly taking out Justine Hillerman's left eye, but landed me bent over, spewing my guts out in the complex parking lot. To say this had not been my finest moment was like saying the Pacific Ocean is reasonably large.

As my life tends to go, Jackson Bennett—quite possibly the most attractive man I've ever encountered in real life let alone shared an apartment building with—had found me on my knees, unable to walk myself back to the party. I still had no idea how I'd gotten to the parking lot in the first place.

In the present moment, I had a choice to make— let Jackson know that it was me once again in need of saving, or hold my tongue and hope someone else came along. A slicing wind whipped through the stairwell, stinging my cheeks, and my answer became immediately clear.

"I'm over here." I hopped into the light, ignoring the heat of embarrassment creeping up my neck. Pointing out the obvious, I said, "I need help."

"Before I get too close," he said, "have you been drinking?"

Vomit on a man's shoes one time and you're

marked for life.

"After last night, I never want to sniff, let alone drink alcohol ever again."

Leaving the warmth of his apartment, Jackson strolled toward me. "You might have been okay if you'd skipped the meat tray."

That explained the chunks of ham I'd found in my hair this morning.

"I would have been better off not letting Katy make my drinks. I'd forgotten she operates on the *more is more* philosophy."

Hopping forward, I lost my balance, waving my arms in the air like a plummeting albatross.

"Whoa, there." My reluctant knight in muted plaid caught me before gravity won out. "We need to get you off this ice."

"If you could help me get upstairs—" I started.

"My place is closer," he argued. "Besides, those stairs are frozen solid."

He was telling me.

I hobbled beside him, leaning against his solid frame, leaving bits of my dignity behind with each hop. Seconds before crossing the threshold, I realized I was about to enter Jackson Bennett's apartment. The moment felt weighty. Like entering the church on your wedding day. Or standing before the Eiffel Tower for the first time.

I'd experienced neither scenario, but felt confident about the analogies.

"Easy now," Jackson murmured, the vibration rolling from his body to mine, distracting me enough to make me forget why I was leaning on him in the first place.

Frazzled, I put weight on my right foot and instantly regretted the foolish move.

"Leaping lizards!" All my weight fell onto Jackson and he lifted me off the ground as if I weighed no more than a wayward puppy leaping into his arms.

Running on instinct, I closed my eyes and buried my face in his neck, breathing hard until the shooting pain subsided, and Jackson's fresh pine scent filled my senses.

"What do you have there?" asked a female voice.

Of course, Jackson Bennett had a girlfriend. And here I was, clinging to her man's neck.

"This is Daphne Wells," he explained, lowering me to the sofa with care. "She lives up on the third floor." Jackson rose to his full height, towering above me, and said, "Explain how this happened."

Feeling as if I'd landed in the principal's office, I regressed a dozen years to the awkward teen I'd once been.

"I fell down the stairs."

"What were you doing out in this weather?"

Reminding myself that I was not a recalcitrant child, I lifted my eyes to find his clear green gaze staring back. "I was taking a bag to the dumpster. I only meant to be out for a couple minutes."

"Do you have any sense of self-preservation?" he asked. "First, you nearly drink yourself to death, and tonight you venture down icy stairs. If I didn't know better, I'd think you lack the will to live."

"Jackson, leave the poor woman alone." The blonde, who oddly enough possessed similar eyes to the man she'd just scolded, eased onto the edge of the couch. "Where does it hurt?" she asked.

I fought the temptation to reply, *my pride*. "My right ankle," I said instead. Wanting to convince someone in the room that I was not a brainless twit with a death wish, I added, "These boots are supposed to be good on ice. I thought I'd be safe for a quick trip down and back up."

"Unless they come equipped with metal spikes, nothing is good on ice," Jackson cut in, earning a stern look from his girlfriend.

"Make yourself useful and hold her hand," she ordered, before shifting a more patient gaze my way. "My name's Josie, and I'm going to ease your boot off as gently as I can, okay? Feel free to squeeze my brother's hand as hard as you need to."

Her brother? That explained the eyes, though the pair bore no further resemblance. Jackson's hair gleamed black as night, while Josie's glowed yellow-gold. Without argument, Jackson kneeled on the floor beside me and took my hand in his. "You need a keeper," he whispered.

I did have a tendency of getting into messes of this nature. Last month, I'd nearly broken my nose at work, thanks to a swinging door assaulting my face. Or rather, my face being in the wrong place at the wrong time. And then there'd been the feline attack last week.

I'd agreed to feed another neighbor's three cats while she visited family out of town. As Mrs. Wollinski had promised, her large orange tabby greeted me with purring enthusiasm, but the owner hadn't mention his tendency to bite the hand that fed him—literally. I was still cleaning the wound daily.

Instead of arguing, I admitted the truth. "Yes, I do."

As Josie unlaced my boot, Jackson tucked a wayward curl behind my ear. "You smell better tonight."

Unsure how to take the compliment, I ignored it. "I really am sorry. I feel bad about your shoes."

He shrugged. "I needed a new pair anyway."

Josie tugged the boot and I winced.

"What the heck are you doing, Josie?" Jackson snapped. "You're hurting her."

The concern in his voice lit a tiny ember in my chest. His hand was soft but strong in mine, and his body heat went a long way to warming me up.

"We're almost there," Josie mumbled, angling the boot so as not to bend my ankle any more than she had to. "Easy now." As my toes cleared the soft leather, my would-be nurse eased a pillow beneath my ankle. "The worst is over now."

Ignoring the woman at my feet, Jackson flashed a crooked grin and continued to hold my hand. "I was worried about you last night."

"You were?" I asked, suddenly shy.

"That's why I followed you to the parking lot. You weren't in any shape to be wondering around in the dark alone." His thumb trailed over the back of my hand, and my mouth went dry.

Clearing my throat, I asked, "Do you know why I went out there?"

Dark brows arched. "You don't remember?"

Jackson was cute, but a terrible bluffer. "Really?"

He laughed. "I withdraw the question. I barely made it into Wilson's apartment when you stumbled by claiming you needed your sunglasses out of your car."

"Wow," I muttered. "I really was sloshed."

"Do you do that often?" His eyes locked on mine.

After a deep breath, I told the truth. "I haven't

had more than two glasses of wine in a night in at least four years. Which explains why four drinks hit me so hard. And the fact that Katy admitted to pouring whiskey, vodka, and rum into each cup."

With a shake of his head, he whistled. "I thought she was your friend."

"You'd have to know Katy to understand. She's a bit twisted, but she's a good person. And she knew I needed to cut loose."

"Here's an ice pack," Josie interrupted. I'd been so focused on Jackson, I hadn't noticed her leave the sofa. "Your right ankle is about twice the size of the left one. I think it's a safe guess that you've broken something."

Great. Because getting up and down three flights of stairs in the dead of winter wasn't already a pain in the butt. Why not add crutches to the mix? And then there was the problem of waiting tables with a bad ankle.

Flinging an arm over my eyes, I sighed in surrender. "I really can't win."

"Accidents happen, Daphne," Jackson consoled. "In six weeks or less you'll be good as new."

"By then, they'll find someone to take my place at the restaurant and I'll be unemployed. Again."

Jackson tapped on the back of my hand. "Don't you have a business degree?"

Now he sounded like my mother.

"Yes, I have a business degree," I replied, cueing up the same speech I'd recited five times in the last two months. "And I spent four month hunting for a job with no luck until it came down to clinging to my pride, or paying my rent. The rent took priority."

After a beat of silence, Jackson said, "Daphne, look at me."

Uncovering one eye, I said, "What?"

"Do you know anything about spreadsheets?"

Blinking, I struggled to figure out when this rescue had turned into a job interview.

"I know spreadsheets forward and backward."

"Then give me a copy of your resume and I'll find you a position."

Leaning up on an elbow, I cringed as the ice pack hit the wrong spot. "You'd do that for me? I mean, you have the *power* to do that?"

With a chuckle, he said, "I'm a headhunter. It's what I do."

For a second there, I thought he'd been offering his help because he liked me. I'd clearly injured my head along with my ankle.

"Besides," he added. "I like you. I want to help you."

Life had dealt me too many blows lately for me not to be suspicious. "You don't even know me."

Jackson shrugged. "I know the drunk you, and she's oddly endearing, despite her profane language."

"Her what?" With a quick shake of my head, I corrected the statement. "My what?"

"You called a fire hydrant the "C" word."

"No," I exhaled, leaning up as much as I could. "I never use that word."

Green eyes went wide. "You did last night. And that was just for starters."

I gripped his hand tighter, failing to register that he'd yet to break contact. "How are you not appalled? I don't remember any of that, but it couldn't have been pretty."

"The language became easy to forgive once you told me that I was, by far, the sexiest guy you'd ever puked on."

Dropping back to the couch, I covered my eyes again, and prayed the couch would swallow me up. "This cannot be happening."

This time, Jackson pulled my arm away and leaned above me.

"Daphne, I've said hello to you at the mailboxes four times, and you've never even made eye contact. I've parked next to your car at every opportunity, hoping we might meet while leaving at the same time. The one time my plan worked, you ducked into your car as if afraid I might accost you." Tapping the tip of my nose, he smiled, revealing two heart-stopping dimples. "I was starting to think you found me repulsive."

Did the man not own a freaking mirror? He was as far from repulsive as a person could be.

"I thought you were just being neighborly and was afraid if I opened my mouth, I'd embarrass myself. You're so far out of my league, Jackson. I mean, you're…" I waved a hand to indicate as much of him as I could from my horizontal position. "You're perfect. And I'm, well, not."

"He is *so* not perfect," Josie interjected, reminding me once again that we were not alone. The woman had ninja level invisibility skills. "He has caveman feet, and if our father is any indication, he'll have hair growing out of his ears in less than five years."

"Hey, Josephina," he said. "How about giving us some privacy?"

"No problem, Jackson Ashley."

I laughed. I couldn't help myself. Jackson Ashley was not a manly name. Though I wouldn't want to go through life as Josephina either. The Bennett parents were either clueless or cruel.

As a door on the other side of the kitchen clicked shut, my rescuer took a seat on the edge of the sofa next to my hip. I pretended the close proximity of our middle regions had no effect on me. I'm sure my shifty eyes revealed the truth.

"I don't agree with my sister often, but she's right. I'm far from perfect. But in my experience, perfect is boring. I'd rather have someone who is unexpectedly clever, mildly bashful, and unwaveringly loyal any day. Deep blue eyes and wild copper curls are a nice bonus."

Afraid to breathe, I stared into his eyes for several seconds, searching for any sign of jest. Any chance that this little speech was nothing more than a cruel joke. But sincerity shone in his jade depths.

"You see all that in me?" I asked.

"Yeah, I do."

Giving into temptation, I trailed my fingers along his jaw line, the scruff sharp against my skin. "If my ankle really is broken, getting up to my apartment is going to be really difficult."

"I know someone on the ground floor who has a spare bedroom," Jackson replied, the naughty grin doing funny things to my insides.

"Doesn't that guy have a sister staying with him?"

"She only came over for dinner."

My bad luck streak sure had taken a turn for the better. But the butterflies in my chest were being smothered by a different sensation further down.

"Is it too early in this relationship to ask a favor?" I said, playing with a button on his flannel shirt.

"I'll do whatever I can."

"Good," I said, gripping the front of his shirt as I

lifted onto my other elbow. "Please take me to the emergency room, because I am in screaming pain."

Jackson leapt to his feet. "Josie, get out here," he yelled. "We're going to the hospital!"

Six hours later, I was back on Jackson's couch, a pink cast weighing down my right foot, and a gorgeous man at my beck and call. As far as tumbles went, this was one I'd gladly take again.

***

BIO: Terri is an Amazon and Wall Street Journal best selling author. In 2012, she was named a finalist in the Romance Writers of America Golden Heart contest for unpublished manuscripts, and she signed with an agent soon after. Since then she has published, through Montlake Romance, four books in the Anchor Island series and four books in the Ardent Springs series, with the fifth book due to be released in May, 2017.

http://www.terriosburn.com/

Witching 101
By K.F. Breene
USA Today Bestselling Author

Jackie stared down at the starter pack spread across the living room floor. Her roommate, Eva, who thought witchcraft was something made-up by J.K. Rowling, was away for the afternoon, thankfully leaving Jackie in peace to concoct her first potion.

Each item from the pack had a letter of the alphabet affixed to it, an absolute must for some of the ingredients, or, how in the world would she be able to tell the difference between an eye of a newt and a fermented spider eye? Granted, the size should be a giveaway, but she wasn't in the habit of staring at eyeballs displaced from the head in which they came.

She shivered. *Eww.*

The medium-sized cauldron was smaller than expected based on the photo online, and it perched on an old, faded rug. As if the whole situation wasn't scary enough, its legs ended in a semblance of iron claws

"It's not scary," she reminded herself. "It's new and different. Exciting. Yes, that's the word." She nodded. "Exciting."

Her roommate, Eva, had thought buying a starter kit online, entitled *Witching 101,* was weird. But where did she think true witches were supposed to start? A graveyard?

Jackie snorted. Preposterous. No, the kit made sense. All the ingredients were clearly labeled and in their right doses. The cauldron even had a plug so you didn't have to light a fire under it. That was very handy.

She picked up the yellowed sheet of paper that looked like a page from an ancient spell book.

"That's a little hokey," she muttered.

Though, if she was being honest with herself, she'd admit that pretending she was reading out of a real spell book was exciting. She could imagine going into her future study, preparing her supplies, and then cracking open a dusty volume filled with advanced spells for only the most experienced witch. She'd be revered in the witching community and have a line of people at her door, waving money at her, desperate for cures to ailments or wanting special potions to capture the eye of a handsome fellow.

Although she'd have to turn down the people asking for a love potion. Making someone feel something against their will was wrong. If she was going to be a witch, she'd have to be an honest one. Ethics in witchery—*ooh, that is a good title for the book I'll eventually write.*

She'd known she was a witch since middle school, feeling a certain warmth inside her that then flowed through her veins, often referred to as women's intuition. But where did people think that intuition originated?

Magic. That's where.

When she would sit in the classroom, listening to the history instructor, and suddenly get a premonition of something *coming,* she didn't listen at first. Even after the first two times of the feeling manifesting in material proof, once getting a sweater in the mail, and another time seeing a very cute friend of her brother's, she chalked it up to coincidence. Two-day delivery and that friend being over often was an easy explanation.

But it kept happening.

She'd get that warmth spreading through her body. The tingles. The knowledge that *something* was about to happen, or was coming, or wasn't right, and finally she could deny it no more.

She had magic.

She also had an affinity for making people laugh when she told them she had magic. That part was annoying.

After years of wanting to explore this natural gift, but too embarrassed to hang out in the New Age store and ask questions, she'd stumbled upon an ad online. *Make your first potion in a matter of minutes*, it boasted, showing a picture of a bubbling pot. *Ever wondered if you have the divine power? Find out now with this witching starter kit, guaranteed to create a real potion or your money back!*

Sure, the ad was a hard sell, targeted at a certain playacting crowd who waved wands and wore robes out in public, but the company had to make money, didn't they? They had to appeal to the hobby-seeker as well as the true witch if they wanted to make a solid *go* at their enterprise. The company seemed like it was just starting out—they needed all the new customers they could get.

She gave a decisive nod. "Okay," she said with a deep breath, feeling more comfortable talking herself through this process. "Let's do this."

The directions seemed easy to follow. Add a set of ingredients, stir in a certain direction, add more, stir in another direction, add the rest, let it bubble, reap the rewards. Simple.

See? She was a natural. These things just came easy to her. When Eva got home, she'd get to sample the potion and benefit from good luck for one day.

Wait.

Jackie squinted at the box.

That's right, they'd been out of the good luck kit. This was for the apathy-inducing potion.

She wasn't sure why she'd want to promote apathy, unless maybe she needed to ask her parents for money. A little indifference as they handed over the needed amount sounded good. She was tired of getting the lecture regarding her irresponsible purchases. If just once she didn't have to defend why she needed to spend part of her weekly allowance on something other than books and food for college, it would be nice.

She bit her lip. This was dangerously close to making someone feel something against their will. Although anti-anxiety pills were similar, weren't they? She bet they probably were.

No matter. This was just a trial run, anyway. She could get the luck potion later. Heck, she could create the luck one herself when she got the hang of this.

"Add three gallons of distilled water," she read aloud.

There was no distilled water among the items in the kit. Shoot.

Tap water would be fine. That was probably what they meant anyway. Why else would they leave it out of the kit?

The water filled a little over half of the cauldron, which made sense, because there were a lot more ingredients to come and bubbling to do. There needed to be plenty of space for everything. She didn't want the mixture overflowing, soaking the rug, and getting on the hardwood floor. Eva had paid the deposit on the apartment.

"Add the blood of three bats, item A." Jackie

eyed the blood in the little vial. It certainly didn't seem like three bats' worth of blood.

Maybe they were just small bats. With watery blood.

She dug her fingernail into the crack between the stopper and the plastic vial, trying to pry the stopper loose. The sucker was on there good and tight. She squeezed, twisted, and pried at the same time. The rubber stopper popped out. A few drops splashed out onto the hardwood floor. She probably should've been standing on the rug for that.

Jackie rubbed the droplets with her socked foot, soaking them up. Then shivered, because she hadn't thought that through, and now had bat blood on her white socks. Whatever… if she expected to be a witch, she'd have to get comfortable with some gross things.

She dumped the blood into the cauldron and watched to see what would happen. Nothing. Not like it would start bubbling right away—it was just blood and tap water at the moment—but still, a little sizzle would've been nice.

"Carefully shake the eye of a newt, item B, out of the package and into the mixture," she read. "Take care not to physically touch the item."

Grimacing, she did as instructed, then followed up with the lovely smelling lavender. Next went in the hemlock root, which didn't look at all like the root she saw online, and finally for this round, the sandalwood.

"Okay, time to stir." She grabbed the large wooden spoon off the ground as she read on. "Using the provided wooden spoon, stir the mixture counterclockwise five times."

It took her a moment of visualizing a clock before she pushed the spoon right. "Oh, wait, no. That's clockwise." Quickly, she reversed directions.

That half stir wouldn't matter. She was still right on track. Besides, it wasn't like she could start over. Buying bat blood and eyes of newts, or any other eyes for that matter, wasn't just a matter of logging onto Amazon. And forget about doing those herself. That sounded as horrible, not to mention it would be extremely hard to find the critters. *Yuck.*

She paused, because she'd forgotten to keep count of her stirs.

It was probably five by now. Or maybe four.

She did one more stir to be sure.

"Okay, next set of ingredients." She slid her finger down the list, then started dumping in items as she verbally checked them off. "Spider eye… check. Snakeskin, yuck. Check. Spotted owl feather—aw, pretty. In it goes. Ground-up bones of a tiger." She *tsked.* "That's just environmentally irresponsible. Those animals are endangered. Hopefully the tiger was already dead."

When the white powder hit the mixture, Jackie finally got her reaction. It fizzled along the surface like a carbonated beverage. The water darkened, now almost the color of the cauldron. A grin spread across her face as she watched, her middle warming and her gut starting to swirl. Tingles spread across her skin.

Her smile slipped.

She was familiar with all the different feelings of her premonitions, and this one was…not great. The sinking feeling generally meant something bad was coming, like a bad grade on a test, or worse, her favorite restaurant was out of meatloaf on Meatloaf Mondays.

Plunk. Plunk. Plunk.

She felt her brow wrinkle as she cocked her head to the side to listen.

Plunk. Plunk. Plunk.

What the heck was that?

The sizzle was starting to dissipate, so she leaned closer to hear.

There was that sound again, like droplets of water hitting a hard surface.

Fear coated her insides as she dropped to the ground. Sure enough, the cauldron was leaking from where the cord attached, near the bottom.

"Shoddy engineering," she said, tearing into the kitchen. "If they would've spent less money on the silly clawed feet, and more on that cord connection, this wouldn't be an issue."

She grabbed a bowl and hurried back before shoving it under the drips. Thankfully, the escaping potion wasn't a fast leak. If she could finish quickly, get it boiling, and bottle it up without delay, she could save the situation.

That explained her bad premonition. She always *knew.*

"Seven stirs, clockwise this time." She pushed the spoon around left. "Dang it!"

Why were clockwise and counterclockwise such a problem for her?

"Five, six…seven. Okay, quickly. Let's see, yarrow root, toadstool— is the toadstool supposed to be dried? Doesn't say. Whatever. They would know, since they put together the kit. A blue rock? Just…a rock? Weird." The rock plunked as it hit the water. "Thyme. Bay leaves. What am I making, a stew? Oh, here we go, frog leg. That does not look like a frog leg. And this definitely doesn't look like a pig's foot. Hmm."

She dropped it in before picking up the final ingredient. The blood of an albino alligator.

"Is that even a thing? I've never heard of an albino alligator." The dripping below the cauldron slowly picked up speed. Feeling the urgency, she dumped the slightly pink blood in, trusting in the potion creators. After all, when she read the instructions out of an old, dusty volume, she'd have to trust the original creators, wouldn't she?

Focusing, she stirred the correct way, the correct number of times, and even reversed when she was supposed to. "I'm getting good at this."

The drips fell faster, one after the other. The leak was getting worse much too quickly.

"I need to get this show on the road." She grabbed the plug and reached toward the outlet. It went taut, pulling on the already loose cauldron connection. A large drop escaped into the waiting bowl below, inky black.

"Donkey crackers, I'm too far away."

No time to lose, Jackie grabbed the rug and pulled. Luckily the pot couldn't have been real iron, because it didn't seem nearly heavy enough. Unluckily, that meant she'd applied way too much strength.

The whole setup jostled her way. Upset potion slopped out the other side, then rolled toward her, hitting the lip and spilling over. She flinched and looked at her arm. An eye looked back.

"Cripes on a cracker, gross!" She flicked it off. Her aim was true, shooting the eye back into the mixture.

Not waiting for all the ingredients to get back into the pot, she plugged the cauldron in. That done, she ran around to the other side to see what escaped. Her foot hit a patch of water and slid away from her.

Mouth rounded in a soundless yell of surprise,

she went sideways before crashing onto the ground. Pieces of plant lay next to her face. Wetness soaked into her leggings. Struggling to her feet, she scooped up the soggy foliage and dumped it back into the cauldron before hunting for more.

How had the pig's foot made it out? Did pig's feet float?

She had no idea, but the thing was on the ground, not in the bowl. That was bad. She was sure she needed it.

A continuous stream of liquid beat against the rug. *The bowl!*

"Oh gross, oh gross, oh gross," she said as she grabbed the leathery item and threw it into the cauldron before running around to the other side. She pushed the bowl under the cauldron and rolled her eyes. She'd forgotten to turn the thing on!

"Stupid," she said, flicking the switch next to the leaky connection. The whole system seemed a bit unstable, but it started to hum, a distinctly electronic sound. That was good. It might leak, but at least it would heat. Everyone knew that heat was a necessity for a good potion.

She ran to the kitchen for a towel, limping slightly. Her hip hurt something fierce. Back in the living room and the mixture had changed to a purple color. That was cool. It was sizzling again, too. Also cool.

"Now we're cooking," she said, noticing the drips had turned into a thin stream of water falling from the cauldron.

"Keep it together, Martha," she said. She hadn't planned on naming the cauldron, but Martha seemed to fit. She'd go with it. "We're nearly there."

She pulled the bowl away, accidentally slopped

dark liquid onto the already saturated rug, and threw the towel under the stream. Hurrying, because whatever was going to happen with the potion would happen soon, she could *feel* it, she dumped the contents of the bowl into the sink. Before turning away, she paused, staring down at the liquid oozing in the sink basin. Did it seem thicker?

It did. She was sure of it. The heat was thickening the liquid into a real potion!

Grinning like a lunatic, she raced back to the cauldron. The towel was saturated now and the rug around it sopping. The floor beneath would definitely be wet.

That wasn't good. The warning on the label said the potion might stain.

Nervous flutters tickled her stomach. She replaced the bowl and felt the side of the cauldron. Hot. The potion couldn't be far from bubbling. And look how thick it was!

Her split-second decision was to press on. If the floor was already wet, another few minutes wouldn't make a difference. Besides, something would surely take out a stain. Another potion, perhaps.

She snatched up the spoon and ran it through the liquid. A dark purple layer clung to the wood. The first bubble popped on the surface. Another followed. The thin stream of liquid coming out the connection enlarged, the leak getting worse.

"C'mon, c'mon," she said, antsy. The bowl was filling up already. She should've gotten a bigger one. In fact, she should've gotten a whole bunch of storage containers to scoop the potion out as soon as it was done.

Speaking of, how would she know it was done? She tried to read the jiggling instructions as she ran back to the kitchen. *The potion will start bubbling, each popping bubble getting more severe, until they sound like mini firecrackers.*

That sounded exciting.

She was to then turn off the heat, let it cool, and her potion would be ready.

After jamming the directions into her back pocket and loading her arms with containers, she turned back toward the living room.

Crack!

Jackie jumped in alarm. The containers rattled in her arms. One broke away and tumbled toward the ground.

Choosing to leave that fallen soldier behind for now, she hurried toward the living room.

Crack! Crack! Crack! Crack!

It was happening!

CRACK!

"That one didn't sound so mini," she said with suddenly harried breath, back on scene.

The bubbles weren't acting like that of a normally boiling liquid. Each one rising to the top was abnormally large, almost covering a quarter of the surface area. When it popped it spat potion out of the cauldron, splashing deep purple across the rug and floor.

"Time to shut it off," she mumbled, grabbing the cord and yanking. The plug ripped from the wall. The connection ripped from the bottom of the cauldron.

A deluge of liquid poured from the new hole, overrunning the bowl and quickly soaking the rug.

CRACK! CRACK! CRACK!

The whole cauldron shook. Huge splashes burst from the pot.

CRACK!

Deep purple splattered the closest wall. A spray of liquid slapped the ceiling. A glob landed on the couch.

"Oh my gosh, what is happening?" With one hand she grabbed a container and tried to catch the liquid streaming from the bottom. With another container she tried to scoop liquid out of the top, ducking along the side so none of the exploding potion attacked her.

CRACK. CRACK.

Those not-so-mini explosions were calming down a little, thank heavens.

A glob hit the TV and slid down the surface before falling to the floor, leaving a streak on the screen. More potion splatter-raked the wall.

"Just stop already, *please*."

She switched out a container on the bottom, moving the full one next to the bowl. In her effort, her face strayed too high.

Crack!

A small burst of potion smacked the side of her face.

"Oh no, my eyes!" She clawed at the stuff, smearing it down her cheek and away from her eyes. Staggering like a drunk at Mardi Gras, she accidentally bumped the bowl and stepped on the full container. Potion slopped over her foot and onto the floor.

Crack.

The volatile potion left in the cauldron began to calm as it cooled.

Eyes okay, Jackie worked to right the container—not that it helped much—and get another going.

Keys jingled in the door.

A thrill of fear shot through her. Half paralyzed with what was about to happen, she straightened up slowly.

Eva walked in carrying a canvas bag with celery leaves sticking out the top. The door closed before Eva glanced up and froze. Her wide-eyed gaze roamed the living room, hitting the still oozing potion now coating half the floor, the ceiling decorated in purple sprays and splats, the TV, the couch…

Eva's stare hit Jackie.

"I can explain how that happened," Jackie said, like a deer caught in the headlights. Suddenly she remembered the apathy-inducing potion. "But first, you have to try this. It's incredible!"

***

BIO: K.F. Breene is the USA Today bestselling author of fantasy, contemporary and paranormal romance novels. The Darkness Series and the Warrior Chronicles have sold over a million copies. Book 6, the final in the Warrior Chronicles, has just released.

http://www.kfbreene.com/

Double Rainbows
by Rayne Hall
Bestselling Author

Gerard hurried down the spiral staircase of Sibyl's lighthouse, his shoes clanking on the metal steps. The blue steel hands of his Rolex showed 8:13. The tide had turned two hours ago, and he did not want to get his new boots wet as he hiked home.

The steep chalk path from the promontory to the seabed was slippery from the night's rain. The sea surface glinted like a diamond-sprinkled sheet, and the air smelled of salty seaweed. In the distance, gulls cackled and squealed.

His chest brimmed with pride at how well he had handled the situation. Telling your girlfriend you would marry someone else required a delicate touch, especially if she was pregnant.

At first, she hurled reprimands. Then she demanded that he leave. But the high tide already submerged the only way out, and she had to let him stay the night. After much coaxing and consoling, her rants subsided to sobs.

Gently, he pointed out that as an artist, she was above conventions like monogamy and marriage, and that single motherhood was all the rage. When he assured her she would remain the love of his life, and promised to continue his Friday night visits, she had stared at him in wide-eyed wonder. By morning, she clung to him with surprising passion.

Sibyl had amazing curves, flaming hair with a temper to match, vivid imagination but little practical sense. She refused to sell the dilapidated lighthouse to one of the wealthy buyers queuing for 'converted character properties,' insisting she loved living surrounded by sea. Isolated when the tide rose twice a day, with only her paintings for company, she lived for Gerard's weekly visits.

Driftwood, whelk eggs and cuttlefish bones littered the low-tide seabed, and bundles of dark bladderwrack lay entangled like scorched spaghetti. As he skirted around chunky boulders, the smell of fishy seaweed grew stronger, wavering between fresh and foul.

Rust-brown shingle and splinters of flint crunched under his fast steps. He had three miles to cover before the incoming tide wet his feet.

In the east, the sun was already painting the sky a brisk blue, but in the north, a curtain of silver-grey rain still veiled the view. A rainbow beyond the promontory framed the lighthouse in bright glory. He squinted. Was that a second rainbow emerging inside the large one? Even as he looked, the faint hues strengthened. Two rainbows, two women – the perfect omen for his fortunate future. Sibyl had probably spotted it already. He pictured her standing at the large window in her round room, paintbrush in hand, plotting to shape the vision into a painting.

But Gerard had no time to linger. The tide waited for no man. Everything about nature – the sun, the rain, the rainbows, the tides – followed complex rhythms, regular but never the same. All was calculable – he patted the tide table in his jeans pocket - yet never quite as expected. Atmospheric pressure, moon phases and such all played a role. Stirred by wind and swelled by the rain, today's sea was already higher than normal.

Waves swished and slurped and rustled across

the shingle. He took firm, even steps past black rocks, across broken shells and white crab corpses. Water ran in thin streams between sand and stones, down the almost unnoticeable slope towards the sea.

Soon he would have both -- a rich wife and an unconventional mistress. A fair man, he would give both women the attention they deserved, but this required skilful planning.

Erica could not be relied upon to show the same flexibility as Sibyl. She might even expect to have her husband to herself.

He had to show tact and not spoil her illusions. A job involving absences from home would help, preferably no longer in her father's employ.

At 8:22, he reached the mainland shore where cliffs towered like steep castle walls. Thirteen feet above, sparse grasses grew in cracks, and gorse shrubs clung to precarious holds. Below that, nothing found a grip on the stark rock face, nothing survived the high tide.

He had another hour and a quarter to walk on the seabed to the end of the cliff that lined the shore. The wind rose, whipped up waves and sculpted them into mountain ridges. Puddles filled, and water streamed into rock pools. With the hem of his shirt, he wiped the thin coating of salt from his spectacles, and squinted at the sea. The tide was coming faster than it should.

An illusion, no doubt, from a water level raised by wind and rain. Today's high tide was at 13:01, which meant the sea did not hit the cliff until 10:30, and then he would be past the inaccessible part and on dry secure land.

He checked his watch again, just in case. The blue steel hands on the silvered dial showed 8:28, as it should. A quick glance back revealed the bill already washed by water, the route he had walked submerged by the incoming tide. Only its tip, the rock with the lighthouse, still pointed like an admonishing finger out of the sea. The rainbow was now clearly a double, its colours sharp.

Ignoring natural laws, the water crawled closer, brushing the scattered rocks with angry lashes and frothy caress. Puddles filled and forced Gerard to take big strides from rock to rock.

He checked the tide table, ran his finger down the column for today's high tide. 13.01. He was right, and had an hour and a half to clear the rest of the cliff.

Was the sun supposed to stand so high at half past eight? All he knew was that it rose from the east. On previous walks, he had not paid it much attention. He always left Sibyl's place at low tide, which was a different time every week, so the sun was never in the same place anyway. Though the sun looked high, and the water was close.

What if his watch had stopped? A Swiss Rolex was supposed to be infallible. *Ticke-tac, ticke-tac, ticke-tac,* the watch assured him, and the minute hand moved another notch.

As the water's edge sneaked nearer, he scanned the cliff face for an escape. Surely there was some gap, some path, some stairs hewn into the rock? But he had walked this route on many Saturday mornings, and knew there was none. Thoughts and fears whirled through his mind, questions, worries and doubts.

A drop of sweat slid down his back, and another. Keeping close to the cliff, he marched faster.

Wall-like waves crashed and shoved sheets of white foam at his feet. Tendrils of panic curled into his stomach while gulls glided past in mocking calm.

A cloud blocked out the sun. The air chilled and pimpled the skin on his arms, even as the sweat of fear pasted the shirt to his back. To his left, the cliff stood smooth, steep, merciless.

Salty splashes stained his shoes, sneaked into his socks, soaked his trouser legs. The drum of fear beat in his chest. With the watch pressed to his ear, he ran.

Boom boom boom, his heart thudded. The watch went *ticke-tac, ticke-tac, ticke-tac* above the hiss of the waves.

The water rose fast. Icy wet snaked around his ankles, his calves. Still the cliff stretched without end.

No one could have reset the watch except last night. Suddenly he could explain how that happened.

Sybil! Sweet Sybil. So grateful. So forgiving.

The next wave slammed his chest against the rock with ice-cold force.

***

BIO: Rayne is the author of the bestselling Writer's Craft guides. She has more than sixty books published under several pen names in fantasy, horror, historical and non-fiction, by several publishers and in several languages. After living in Germany, China, Mongolia and Nepal, she has settled on the south coast of England where she enjoys gardening and walking along the seashore.

http://www.raynehall.com/

Intruder
by Caroline Grace
Previous CWI Contest Winner

Jen was babbling. She knew it, but couldn't stop. "Some guy I've never met sent me a Facebook friend request, and I think he might be kind of cute. You ever hear of Lincoln Webber? Lincoln's kind of a cool name. Cool names belong to cool guys, right?" She paused for a breath and a beauty check, pulling down the passenger side visor. Smokey eyes with long black lashes looked back at her.

"Uh... no. Do I have to remind you about your last cool-name guy? Traxler was a loser. And totally possessive! Every time you got a text, he had to know what it was about. How do you not remember this?" Rachel was a direct, no-nonsense kind of woman, and Jen was just easy-going enough not to care. Their unique recipe for friendship had worked since sixth grade.

"Traxler's still my friend, and you know he's going to be at the party tonight."

"Yeah, he's still in love with you, Jen, and you know it. Be careful with him."

"Maybe in lust... I could believe that. I'm not sure love was ever involved. Oh, wait, stop! You just went by it! Turn around and go back!"

Instinctively Rachel slammed on her brakes and tires squealed. "Geez Louise, Jen! Take a breath once in awhile! You said it was a long way before we turned."

"Whatever, sorry. That was the turn."

Rachel maneuvered the Jeep into a u-turn at the

next cross street, doubling back to The Everglades, a series of white pitched party tents of varying heights. Multi-colored party lights illuminated the Welcome Dock attached to the front tent. A chocolate fountain and complimentary champagne enticed the unsuspecting. Rachel swung into the first open spot she found.

"Hey, Rach, I want to look at this guy's Facebook page before we go in. Don't get out yet," Jen's voice stalled out, and her face froze, but her eyes kept moving back and forth across the phone screen. "That's weird. That can't be right. Look at this."

"What? So he's kind of cute... well okay, and he's got a rockin' body. Let's go in now."

"No, hang on, something's not right with this picture. I'll make it bigger... oh my gosh!" Goose bumps formed all over Jen's body, and she could feel the hairs on her arms stand straight up. She felt like all the air had been squeezed out of her body, and her voice came out soft and low. "This is my kitchen, Rachel. This man, Lincoln--in his Facebook cover photo, he's standing in my kitchen and I've never seen him before."

"Wait, what? He's in your kitchen? Are you sure? That can't be right. Surely, you must know him or else it's not your kitchen. That's the only way that could've happened."

"No!" Jen's tone was escalating, "Did you not hear me? I've never seen this man before in my life! And it *is* my kitchen. Look, there's the cabinet door that's missing a handle. And look at the frig door -- that's my stuff on the door." The implications of Jen's new reality soaked in and showed in her wide-open eyes. "Oh my gosh, Rachel. How is he in my house? What am I going to do?"

"Okay, okay... let's go in. It'll take your mind off things. We'll figure this out. We're just missing something, that's all."

That being the only good option at the moment, Jen nodded and stepped out of the Jeep.

They picked their way up to the Welcome Dock, a slight breeze blowing Rachel's hair across her dark eyes.

Jen grabbed two champagne flutes, chugging their contents like a frat boy, then daintily dabbing her red lips with a party napkin.

"Are you sure you should do that on an empty stomach?" Rachel whispered.

"Yep. Oops…" Jen covered her mouth as a belch escaped. "It's the quickest way I know to feel better. Hey, that's him – the Facebook guy in my kitchen! He's over there!" Then, rather too loudly, "Lincoln, I see you – come back here!"

"I don't see him," Rachel said. "Oh, that's not even him! Wait, Jen… you can't run in those shoes."

But Jen had already come to a full stop. "Where did he go? I know I saw him. He was over there in the next tent. I know he was." Jen wiped furiously at the tiny rivulet rolling down her right cheek.

"Come on, sweetie. Let's hit the bar. Someone said it's in the second tent over there. What's it called?"

Jen brightened considerably. "It's the Palisade… only the best bar in the whole complex!"

Two sets of 4-inch heels attached to long legs and generally beautiful bodies strolled their way to the bar with practiced ease. Hearing their approach, a well-muscled man at the bar turned toward them, grinning from ear to ear, "Ladies. Good to see you!"

"Geez, let's go, Jen." Rachel grabbed Jen's arm,

wheeling her around.

"No!" Wresting her arm away, Jen turned back toward the bar.

"Not me. I'm out of here," and Rachel drifted away solo through the crowd.

Jen faced her ex. "Traxler, how are you? I'm actually glad to see you!"

"What's up with that? No, don't tell me. I'll take it any way I can get it. You're lookin' good, babe."

The way Traxler's eyes scrutinized Jen made her squirm.

"If I had my camera set-up with me, I'd be tempted to do a photo-shoot right now... you in that tight red dress, blue eyes, blonde hair pulled up, except for this little strand right here." His hand reached out for the errant tendril of hair.

Jen was almost swept away again. She pulled up a bar stool, and, teasing Traxler a little, she avoided eye contact until she finished ordering her drink. "Chocolate martini, please." Turning full face to Traxler, she bestowed a smile on him, "Hey, can I ask you something?"

"Anything. And the answer is *yes*."

Jen pushed away an errant hand on her knee. "I see you've already been drinking."

"Just waitin' on you."

"You didn't even know I was coming."

"I know everything about you. Don't forget that." Traxler's smile was wicked and enticing at the same time. "Cigarette?" he asked, reaching into his pocket.

"Stop it. You know I don't smoke. Seriously, I need to ask you something. Do you know this guy? His name is Lincoln Webber," Jen handed Traxler her cell phone.

"No, why? You need me to get rid of him?"

"Seriously, look at this picture, Trax. He's in my kitchen! Explain how that happened!" She pulled the phone back, and stared at it. "Something about him looks familiar, but I can't put my finger on it."

"Don't know him. You want me to stay over with you a couple of nights?"

"Absolutely not! I'll be fine." As much as Jen hated to admit it, she wasn't sure she could withstand Traxler's advances if he stayed over, and, judging by the smirk on his face, he knew it. "I can see this conversation isn't going anywhere. I'll see you, Trax." She pushed a large tip across to the bartender. As she slid off her stool, her dress inched up her thigh.

Traxler didn't miss it. Before Jen could retrieve her drink, he grabbed her and slapped a hot kiss on her lips.

Pulling away, she paused long enough to reclaim her drink, turned deliberately and strode away. She didn't have to look back to know Trax was grinning and watching her move. She found Rachel in Tent #4, The Twilight, which featured the only dance floor in the complex.

Three dances and two drinks later, under great protest from Rachel, the pair made their way back to the Jeep.

"Okay, Rachel, I do my best thinking when I'm buzzed. Are you okay to drive, 'cause I have lots to say?"

"I'm fine. You yanked me away before I finished my first drink." Rachel pushed her hair back and gave Jen a searing look.

"Well, you don't have to be snippy about it. Anyway, listen... what about that guy that moved in a couple of houses down? Could it be him? I've only met him once, and I can't really remember what he looks like."

"His name's Todd or Tim or something, though, isn't it?"

"Well, of course this nut job's not going to use his real name!"

"If your stalker was a girl, I'd for sure know who it was," Rachel laughed, trying to break the tension. "Do you remember Helena Hennessey that used to date my brother, Brian?"

"Oh my gosh, yes! Didn't she sneak a copy of his house key and his car key?"

"Yeah, remember she was inside his house waiting for him to get home, and then later she stole his car!" Rachel laughed again, "It took him almost a year to dump her, and he ended up finally getting a restraining order before she left him alone! Last I heard she was trolling dating websites for her next victim!"

"Rachel, seriously, I have to figure this out or I might never sleep again. So, about the guy who just moved in down the street... why couldn't it be him?"

"Okay, okay, just trying to lighten the mood! I don't know, it just seems kind of chancy to do something like that to someone who lives so close to you. And why? Wouldn't you be afraid you'd be recognized? But how about this…. what if Lincoln had some connection to the girl you bought the house from? I mean, think about it… you've been there less than a year, and she was a single girl, right? What about that?"

"I guess that could be a lead, but how do you find that out? You just look up her name, knock at her door, and ask how many guys have ever been in her kitchen?" Jen's fuzzy mind regrouped, "Wait, that won't work anyway. The frig in the picture is the one I brought with me when I moved in, and you saw all my magnets on it. It's happened since I lived there."

Jen put down her window and the crisp night air restored some clarity, "So, I'm thinking, what about someone at work? There's this guy, Daniel, on the 3rd floor in the IT department that calls me all the time. He knows things that go on down in my area, and things about me -- things he shouldn't know. I barely remember what he looks like. I've only seen him like twice, from a distance. But I know his name isn't Lincoln. Of course, he might not use his real name on Facebook. But the funny thing is, I could swear there's something familiar about that Lincoln guy in the picture. For the life of me, I can't figure what it is. Hey, are you awake over there?"

"Just waiting for you to wind down," Rachel said. "About Daniel, stuff gets around at work – that doesn't mean he's the guy. It just means he listens to gossip. Jen, none of them are your guy. What if Lincoln is really a creeper, someone you don't know?"

"Great, creep me out, then drop me off at home alone. I do have that little 22-caliber with the pink grips, I guess."

"I remember you went to the shooting range and actually got pretty good! But could you really hurt someone with a pink 22? That doesn't sound right!"

"I don't know, but I'd sure scare them."

"Jen, are you really okay? We're here, and I kind of hate to leave you."

"I'm good. Gotta gun. See ya, Rach."

Jen heard the sound of gravel crunching under Rachel's tires as she stepped inside her front door. She immediately knew something was wrong, and she knew Rachel was already gone. She stopped cold in the foyer until she could identify the problem. Someone had been smoking in her house. She stood stone-still, listening until she felt certain she was alone.

Jen kicked her shoes off and glided noiselessly across the great room to the utility room. She opened the closet door gently, reached up and found the cold, hard steel of her pink 22. A little braver now, she made her way methodically through the house. Everything seemed in order until she came to the kitchen. She gasped and stopped to take in the sight. All her upper cabinet doors had been pulled off their hinges, and were lying in a heap on the floor. It was an odd moment for calm and logic to kick in, but Jen was grateful for it. She laid the 22 on the kitchen table, pulled her cell phone out of her jacket pocket, and began snapping pictures of the damage.

She sat down at the kitchen table and tried to assimilate this new information. What sense did it make? There was no denying it now; someone had been in her house, and very recently. She couldn't shake the feeling of doom settling over her. Physically and emotionally worn out, she made a call. On the first ring, Rachel's voice came reassuringly through the speaker, "What? I'm coming back to get you. You're okay, right?"

"Do you mind terribly? You didn't get too far, did you? I'll tell you when you get here, but hurry, okay?" Jen pulled out a small overnight bag, laying the gun on the bed while she packed. She threw a wrinkle-free dress in the bag, and glanced at her shoes. They would work with the dress for tomorrow. Make-up, fresh bra and panties, a hair pick, and a toothbrush rounded out the quick packing job. She looked in the mirror, deciding the earrings she had on went okay with the dress.

The doorbell rang, and Jen nearly jumped out of her skin. Looking through the peephole, gun in hand, she yanked the door open, "Sheesh, Rach, you scared me to pieces. You could've just texted me that you were here."

"Thought you might need some help. And you're welcome."

"Sorry, I'm just a little jumpy. I'll be right back with my bag." Silently blessing her concealed carry permit, she threw her gun in her purse, and grabbed her bag. "Thanks again, Rach. I'm ready." One final glance around the room, and Jen pulled the door shut. Safely in the car, she made a decision, "I'm calling the police."

"Did he take something?"

"No."

"Did he hurt you?"

"No."

"Did he break in?"

"No. I don't know how he got in, but there were no broken windows or doors."

"So what will the cops do? Absolutely nothing. There's no dead body on your floor, so they're going to be worthless."

Knowing Rachel was right, Jen didn't bother to answer. Fifty minutes later, Jen was snuggled into Rachel's big fluffy guest bed, searching for sleep. Something was nagging at her about Lincoln's picture... something... what was it? She tossed all night, dreaming dreams she was glad she couldn't recall the next morning. But in between the dreams, she'd somehow arrived at a new conclusion.

She tried her idea out on Rachel in the car the next morning, "So, I'm thinking I might get a home alarm system so I could at least feel safe at night."

"Good idea, but that's gonna be pricey."

"Maybe not so much. Susan, at my work, got a really good deal on one. I'm not sure how much it is monthly, but whatever it is, it would be worth it." Three phone calls and ten hours later, Jen was the proud owner of a security system that alarmed both doors, her sliders, and her bedroom windows. Glad to be sleeping in her own bed that night, Jen had just slipped into her nightgown when the phone rang. Her ex. She decided not to answer, but changed her mind, and snatched the phone up on its last ring. "Hey, Trax."

"What's up, beautiful?"

"Wrapping things up for the night. How about you?"

"Just checking on you. Did you find your mystery guy?"

That was all the encouragement Jen needed. Her words wanted to gush out, but something made her hold them back, "No, but I think he found me again. When I got home from The Everglades last night, he'd been in my apartment and, get this, he took all my kitchen cabinet doors off their hinges. I have no idea why? Does that make any sense to you?"

"Did you call the police?"

"No, Rachel made a good point. There's no dead body on my floor, nothing was missing, and I couldn't even tell how he got in, so they aren't going to do anything."

"I make it a general rule never to agree with Rachel, but, as much as it pains me to say it, she may be right about the cops." Traxler paused, but Jen didn't bite so he went on. "Babe, you do know I can fix those cabinets, right? That's the kind of stuff I do at work every day. I'm off on Thursday. Want me to take a look at them?"

"I won't be home. That's my late day at work."

"Well... do you want to leave me a key, and when you get home, they'll all be done? Now, you might find a naked man on your bed when you get there, but your cabinets will be done."

Too tired to object, Jen answered with a giggle, "I have to go now, Trax, but I'd love it if you could fix my cabinets. There might be a case of craft beer in it for you. Do you remember where I keep my spare key just underneath the angel fountain on the front porch? When you get done, just leave the key inside on the kitchen table. I'm thinking hide-a-key is not such a good idea anymore anyway."

Thursday rolled around quickly, and Jen found herself powering through her work day with a laser focus she seldom had these days. "It's amazing what a good night's rest will do for you," she said to no one in particular. As she was responding to emails, her cell phone rang. Traxler again. "Trax, what's going on?" But she already knew. She could hear the sound blaring in the background. She had forgotten he was coming over.

"You didn't tell me you were going to set your alarm and it's going off right now. All your neighbors are staring at me, so could you hurry up and tell me what to do? And maybe call off the police if they're going to come out?"

"I'm so sorry! I completely forgot about that. Go to the keypad in the laundry room. Hit 9068, then hit enter. I'll call the alarm company right now." Jen looked around her, realizing she had spoken more loudly than she intended. It seemed everyone was listening, and she desperately hoped no one was committing her security code to memory.

As she hung up with the alarm company on her cell phone, her desk phone began to ring. Daniel from IT on the third floor. Just thinking of him made her skin crawl. His timing was uncanny. Making herself face her unreasonable anxiety, she picked up the phone. "What can I do for you, Daniel?"

"So what was that all about -- the 9068 and the police and all?"

Her mouth went dry and her mind spun, "What?"

"You know... what's going on down there?"

"I don't know what you're talking about, Daniel. What can I do to help you?"

"Oh, nothing much. You just did! Have a good day, Jen." The phone disconnected.

Jen looked around frantically to see who was watching and listening, and who might be able to shed some light on the call from Daniel. "Susan?"

The young woman in the next cubicle leaned around the partition in response to Jen's query.

"Susan, how could Daniel be upstairs and know about a conversation I just had on my cell phone? He's not even on this floor."

Susan's response was far from what Jen hoped to hear, "I don't know for sure, but I can tell you what I've heard. See those cameras up there?"

Jen nodded. Everyone knew this floor was under constant surveillance due to the nature of the business conducted here.

"Well, I heard that the IT department can turn on microphones in those cameras whenever they want. Everyone kind of knows that Daniel's got a thing for you. He could've turned those mics on whenever he wanted."

"Great…" Jen moaned aloud.

Two hours later, Jen traded in the long workday for an evening at home. Walking in her front door, her home greeted and embraced her for the first time in over a week. No cigarette smoke, no damage to her house, no evidence that anyone had been there in her absence. No one except Traxler, that is. He had come and gone, leaving his mark on her cabinet doors. Jen smiled to herself. He really did do nice work, even if he *was* an eternal flirt. One more good reason not to trust herself around him, she decided. But he still deserved a thank-you.

Trax picked up on the first ring. "Babe! So how's it look?"

"Thank you so much! I owe you a case of beer, you know. You really do good work!"

"I won't say no to the beer, but you know there's something I want more…" his voice trailed off, low and sexy.

"Sorry. Thanks for rescuing a lady in distress, but 'thank you' ends with beer this time."

"A guy has to try, right? I mean there you were all scared about the cigarette smoke, and the cabinets, and Lincoln's Facebook invitation. Face it, Babe, you need me!"

Jen froze, her mind reeling. It was all coming together now. "I didn't tell you about the cigarette smoke, Trax."

"Sure you did, the same night you told me about the cabinet doors." Fear was in his voice.

"No, I absolutely did not. I know why that picture looked so familiar. It's you, Traxler. You're Lincoln. Don't even try to tell me you're not. I don't know how you did it, but that body and those clothes belong to you. I don't know whose face you put on there, but it's you."

"Okay, Babe, just don't hang up. Hear me out… please! It was all for you. So, here's the truth. I still love you. I want you back. I figured if I could help you, make you need me, you'd realize you still loved me, too. I photoshopped my buddy's head on my body, and I knew you'd recognize your kitchen and be a little freaked out. I left the smoke trail at your house on purpose for the same reason. The cabinets… well, that was because I knew I could sweep in and be your hero. It's something I knew I could fix. Babe, it made you need me. I was going to tell you when the time was right. I promise. I really was."

"And you tricked me into telling you my alarm code! You did that on purpose. When were you going to use that to scare me again, huh? Listen carefully, Trax, because I've never meant anything more in my life… don't *ever* call me again."

Jen hung up the phone and immediately called Rachel. "Hey, Rach, are you in the mood for a drink? Right now, my treat. Meet me at the Windsor, in maybe 30 minutes? I'm okay, but I need to talk to you."

An hour later, Jen had spent all her words, and both women were feeling giddy with relief. "Okay, so I have just three things I want to do, then I can put this all behind me."

"What can you possibly need to do? As much as I dislike Traxler, he's harmless. It's over, so let it go."

"Watch and listen, Rachel," and Jen's fingers ripped off a text in flash time. "Okay, here's the text. It's to Traxler and it says, 'I want to talk this out in person. Meet me at the Palisade, Tuesday at 8:00. Wear that black and gray shirt I always liked. It'll help your case. LOL!'"

"No, stop! Don't do it, Jen!"

"Watch and listen, Rachel," Jen said again, as she pushed SEND. "Item number two. A call to one of the attorneys I know. He works in my building." Jen paused long enough to dial her phone. "Hey, Greg, it's Jen from the second floor at I.C.E. Limited. Can you call me tomorrow when you get in? I need a restraining order delivered on Wednesday, and I could use a little help. It can't go out until Wednesday, though. Thanks, Greg."

Jen simply held up her hand when Rachel started to speak. "One more thing, Rachel." A quick Google search, then Jen dialed the phone again, "Hi! Is this Helena? Helena Hennessey? Hey, my name is Jen, and I think you know my friend, Rachel Surrey, and her brother, Brian." Jen paused, listening. "Yes, she is very nice, and she spoke highly of you as well." She rolled her eyes, continuing in spite of Rachel's frantic hand gestures indicating she should hang up.

"Yeah, I'm sorry things didn't work out with Rachel's brother. You're right, I think every girl should have a key to her boyfriend's house and car. I would've done the same thing." Jen was shaking her head violently, and Rachel was slapping the table, hardly able to hold in her giggles.

"Well, the reason I'm calling is because another of my friends, Traxler, saw your profile on a dating site and he really wants to meet you. He's just a little shy, so I told him you and I had a mutual friend, and I would give you a call. Are you up for meeting him? I would take it as a personal favor if you would."

Now Rachel was holding in a belly laugh so big that it was sending tears down her cheeks.

Jen continued. "He said Tuesday at 8:00 at the Palisade would be good. Does that work for you? He said he would wear a gray and black striped shirt. Between you and me, just look for the guy with the smokin' hot body. I'd recognize that body anywhere, even if you photo-shopped someone else's head on it. That's how hot it is! You're going to really like him. He lives over on the north side of the lake on Jefferson and he has a shiny, new, black Escalade. I've driven it. He might let you, too. He's really good at repairing things like broken cabinets and such."

Rachel's head was down on the table now, her body shaking so violently that the whole table was moving.

"No, I'm glad to do it. He really likes surprises, and he loves it when a woman takes control. You're really going to like him. Have a great date Tuesday!" The second Jen ended the call, she erupted in laughter and threw her hand in the air for a high-five from Rachel. "That should keep him occupied for a while! You know what they say about payback!"

Both women ordered another drink.

***

BIO: Caroline Grace is a banker by day and a writer by night. In October, 2012, she was diagnosed with Parkinson's Disease. Writing is her therapy on bad days and her reward on good ones. She enjoys reading, gardening, cooking and making up recipes.

Harry and Margaret
by Randa Sansing
Previous CWI Contest Winner

Back in the mid-1950's in rural Alabama, there were
two hound dogs, Harry and Margaret – named after
the President of the United States, Harry Truman, and
his daughter, Margaret. Long, sleek, and black, they
were beautiful dogs, and I loved them.

Unfortunately, Daddy bought them to be hunting
dogs. Barely past the puppy stage, they didn't know a
thing about hunting. I was only seven years old and
had a soft spot for every animal I'd ever met, so I
couldn't imagine hunting one down, killing it, and
calling it fun.

By the time Daddy took the two dogs on their
first squirrel hunt, they were my pets, following along
at my heels everywhere I went. Poor Daddy had five
girls and nobody to hunt with, so he usually went
alone.

Heading toward the woods with Daddy early one
Saturday morning, the dogs kept turning around,
looking at me, and running back, wanting me to go,
too. I finally had to go back to the house so the dogs
would follow him.

In a few minutes, I heard the loud boom of the
shotgun, followed by frantic, terrified yelps. In a little
while Daddy came back alone, and a couple of hours
later the dogs sneaked back. They were happy to see
me, but when they saw Daddy, they ran under the
house and hid, scared out of their wits.

Daddy discussed the problem with a neighbor
who suggested tying the dogs to a tree and shooting

the gun to help them get used to the sound of gunfire. Daddy decided to try it with Harry first.

While he conducted this experiment, I stayed in the house, lying on the bed face down with cotton in my ears and a pillow over my head. I had never known Daddy to be cruel, but he was torturing the dogs. The experiment not only didn't work, but when the gun fired, Harry broke the chain and streaked for the road. It was several hours before he came slinking home.

Since desperate times call for desperate measures, Dad loaded up the dogs and took them to Uncle Morris, who was considered an expert and knew how to break dogs for hunting. He trained the dogs for several days and sent them home.

On Saturday morning, Daddy left home while it was still dark to join Uncle Morris who lived in the country. I didn't wake up when he left and was still asleep when he returned. As I opened my eyes, he was quietly tiptoeing into the bedroom where I slept with my sisters, and motioned for me to come with him.

"We need your help to find the dogs," he said.

Half asleep and still wearing my nightgown and no shoes, I climbed into the passenger seat of the car. He pulled over and stopped when we got to a big open field close to my uncle's. The field was almost waist high in weeds.

"They ran in there when I fired the gun," Uncle Morris said. "Call 'em and see if you can get 'em to come out. I'll hide behind the car, and you persuade 'em to get in before they see me."

That was the day I learned Daddy had no intention of hurting them. His heart was set on making hunting dogs out of them, and I had no choice but to help.

Feeling like a traitor, I knelt at the edge of the

field.

With the sun just peeping over the mountain, it was still barely daylight. Dew sparkled in the weeds and brush, with a layer of fog hanging above. I began to call softly.

"Come 'ere, Harry, come 'ere, Margaret. Come, girl. Come to me, boy. Come on now. Come 'ere."

I heard a rustling sound and saw the two hounds come out of the brush, wagging their tales, crawling on their bellies, too afraid to stand up. I held out my arms, and they bounded into them, covering my face with wet kisses, and almost knocking me over. It was a happy reunion as I fell back in the grass and played with them for several minutes.

Their tales almost wagged their bodies as they followed me to the car, but they looked unsure as we approached the car. I tried and tried to coax them into the back, but they wouldn't budge so I climbed in first, patted the seat, and called them. Finally, they hopped in. Harry landed in my lap and Margaret squeezed as close as she could get.

Daddy shut the door with haste and we thought the problem solved… until Daddy got in the front seat.

The dogs tried to bolt. The back of the car became a whirl of legs, tails, and toenails trying to scratch their way out through the rear and side windows. It took a lot of cajoling, patting, and rubbing for me to get them settled back down.

Back at home, they jumped out of the car and ran under the house again. At least they were home, and I was relieved we didn't take them back to Uncle Morris. I shuddered to think what his next plan might be.

The next afternoon, I was on the porch watching Harry and Margaret roll around in the grass when

Daddy came out and stood beside me. I stiffened when he said, "Them dogs ain't never gonna be worth anything."

"No, sir. I guess not." My blue eyes must have been as big as saucers as I waited for the next few words.

"I reckon you wanna keep 'em anyhow."

"Yes, sir! I love 'em."

"Well, they're yours."

Nobody ever tried to make Harry and Margaret hunt again. In fact, Daddy didn't hunt much after that either. I often wonder if he really enjoyed it about as much as they did.

Not long after that, the neighbor ambled over while I was playin' with my dogs.

"I thought your daddy took them dogs to be broke so's they'd hunt," he said. "And now he don't go huntin' no more. Seems to me he's the one that got broke of huntin'." He scratched his beard and said, "Explain how that happened."

I just busted out laughing.

***

Same Time Next Year
by Carol White
CWI Contest Finalist 2016

Christine sat in one of the rickety ladder-back chairs at the dining table. The table was scarred after years of neglect, mainly from honeymoon couples who'd carved their initials into the hard maple – like she and Luke had done.

She thought about their beautiful wedding day and her two closest friends, Grace and Chloe, who were her bridesmaids. Since it was a summer wedding, the girls had worn strapless gowns with matching shawls for the church ceremony and then danced the night away.

Christine's wedding dress had been her late mother's and when her father gave her away, there were tears in his eyes when he pulled the veil back. The perfect day continued with a fun-filled reception, and a raucous after-party for the bride and groom, their attendants and friends.

She and Luke fell into bed toward the early hours of the morning, too exhausted to make love. There would be plenty of time for that in the following years, the years that never happened.

She waited for him now as she had done in the past on the exact date of what would have been their fifth anniversary, and he had never disappointed her. Would he still care enough to come five years after the honeymoon that began so joyously but ended in tragedy?

"Christine, you're here," Luke said, almost as a question as he walked into the cottage.

"Happy anniversary, darling. Of course, I'm here. I was wondering if you'd come this year," she said.

"The funny thing is I wasn't sure if *you* would come."

"How could I not?" Christine said. "Today would have been our fifth, you know, and we're always together for our anniversary. Remember how shocked we were that first year, that you could actually see me?"

"Of course I remember, but I didn't know if it'd be the same this time," he said without smiling. "Things change, Christine."

"Not my love for you," she said. "Or this old summer house. Look, our initials are still here. I guess the owners must have a soft spot for lovers because they've never sanded down the table. I always think back to our honeymoon."

"Who could forget it? We thought we'd be totally alone, then all those fishermen passed by the cottage every morning on their way to the dock," he said. "Remember the guy who poked his head through the window to ask if we had any fresh coffee? It's a good thing we were up and dressed for our swim." Luke chuckled, just thinking about it.

"I remember. What little time we had before the accident was wonderful," Christine said, as she traced their initials with a slender finger.

"I know. It was blissful… until the drowning. I've never forgiven myself for that." Luke stared out the window in disgust." It shouldn't have happened."

"It wasn't your fault, darling. No one could have helped."

"I should have seen it coming – been more aware of the rip tides," Luke said. "But, that was five years ago. We need to put it in the past."

Christine walked to his side. Her head drooped in sorrow. "You're right. I don't like to think about it. We only have a few hours. Let's talk about us and our lives together. Do you think we would have had children?"

"You were the love of my life, but our life together is over. It was over five years ago after the accident. I've accepted it, and you must also or neither of us will ever be at peace," Luke said, a little more sternly.

"But at least we have our anniversary, the one day we're somehow able to share."

"Christine, we have to talk about that… about my coming here each year."

"It's not a problem, is it? We both manage."

"It's not a question of managing. It's a question of moving on," he said.

"I don't understand. I thought this was as important to you as it is to me."

"I never thought I'd see you again. Then on our first anniversary I decided to come here. The last thing I expected was to see you. Explain how that happened," he said.

"One of those great mysteries of life after death," Christine said.

Luke paced while gathering his thoughts. He had to make her understand. "That's what we need to talk about. Life, not death," he said.

"What we need is to come here every year, like we've been doing for the past five years. It's the only time we can be together and talk about… about…" Her voice trailed away.

"About what might have been?" he said to finish her sentence. "We can't go back."

She looked him straight in the eye. "Have you stopped loving me?" She sank into the chair, afraid of the answer. "I'll never stop loving you. You'll always be in my heart. I'll never forget our wedding. You were the only man for me then, and now. That can't and shouldn't end just because an accident ended our life together."

"No one could have predicted the drowning that day, least of all me. I was a strong swimmer, but the current was ferocious. I tried to reach you but I couldn't make it in time. I know this sounds trite, but there's a whole world out there for us, Christine. Yes, it's a different world, but there has to be something for each of us."

"Maybe for you. The whole thing is unfair. We only had two weeks. We didn't even get to celebrate our first anniversary. That's why I keep coming back. Don't you see? We found each other again, if only for one day a year. It ties us together," she said.

He shook his head. "What ties us together is weakening. It'll end up pulling us apart."

Christine tried to stay focused, though her energy was beginning to wane. "I don't want it to weaken. Please say you'll keep meeting me. Is it difficult for you to get here?" she asked, almost as an afterthought.

"I'll come as long as you need me, but think about what I've said. You'll never be at peace if you don't accept my death. Neither of us will be."

"Luke, even if you're right, it's still the one day I'm able to look forward to. There's nothing else for me. Is there for you?" she asked.

"I don't know. But as long as we meet, I'll never find out," he said.

"You want to be free, is that it?" she said.

"No. It's just logical. We can't go back. We must go forward." Luke's tone softened as he tried to explain his feelings. It was for her own good. "Are you willing to try it?" he said.

"Not meeting? I can't quit thinking about all this," she said, opening her arms as if to embrace the cottage.

"All what, Christine? Look around. The place is falling down around us. It'll be sold or rebuilt sooner or later, and we won't be able to meet here anyway. You're putting too much pressure on yourself and the past. Let go."

"It's the one place where we were together. I won't let them tear it down," she said, her voice growing louder and more forceful.

"Sweetheart, you're not listening. We can't meet again."

Moisture filled her eyes as she played with a hankie. Without Luke, everything would be lost. She spoke, her voice low. "And what will happen to me if I don't have this day to look forward to? Time will have no meaning anymore," she said.

"I don't know what the future holds for either of us, but we must let it come."

"But without the past I won't be able to feel anything at all. It's like I'm the one who…" she murmured, before Luke broke in.

"I know what you're going to say! You feel like you're the one who died, but you're not. I'm the one who drowned five years ago. You have to stop thinking the accident ended your life. I saw you standing on the shore waving me in, but I couldn't make it. I came today to set you free. You're the one who's alive. You must learn to live. For both our sakes, let go, honey."

"If I let go, how will I know what happens to you?"

Luke laughed and started to fade from sight. "It's like you said. The living will never understand everything about death. You'll find out in your own way, about sixty or seventy years from now. I want you to find love again. It will happen if you let it. And you must set me free to rest in peace. That would be the best anniversary present you could give me," he said, drifting away.

"I'll do that for you," she said. "Please don't go. Stay a while longer."

"I can't stay. Do it for yourself," he said. "Not for me. Please, promise me that."

Christine rose and strained to see her love one last time. "I promise," she said, stretching out a hand and stepping toward the mist. "I'm going to drive back into town now."

The mist was gone.

She stepped to the door, looked out on a fresh new world and said, "It won't be easy, Luke, but you're right. It's time to start over." She pulled her phone from a pocket to arrange a dinner date with friends.

***

Bean Counter
by Dianne Bown-Wilson
CWI Contest Finalist 2016

"A leopard never changes its spots," Mum used to say with a resigned pursing of her lips. But since that night, she's never said it again.

Dad, the butt of her observation, is a typical accountant -- steady, pragmatic, controlled. Whether that was his nature and he chose his profession to fit, or his work reigned in what was once a more reckless disposition, I can't decide.

"Oh, he's always been like that," Mum says. But thirty-five years on, perhaps today's reality has driven out all memory of any rashness in his peppered younger life. After all, she must have thought him exciting at one time.

A few years back, Dad's advertising agency, established some twenty years before, was about to go under. The reason was simple. Brian, his best friend, co-founder and creator, the yang to Dad's yin, had been diagnosed with cancer.

Of course, Dad maintained the status quo and carried on as best he could through the months that Brian went downhill. He wouldn't insult a dying man by taking away his living, but a year or so after the diagnosis, Brian died. A few months later, rather than lose everything and put people out of work, Dad reluctantly agreed to merge with another firm. The company was a long-term rival and he would be working alongside Elwin, its head, a man with whom he'd had few dealings.

"That Elwin is one…" was a phrase that

prefaced many sentences in the ensuing months.

Not that I was generally there to hear the full story, but frequently, in his calls to me, whenever I asked "How's work?" that's how he'd start. I was curious to meet this Elwin. From what Dad said, Elwin was a typical salesman spiced up with a fistful of charismatic flamboyance. "He's a big I–am, irritating as all get out, but good at what he does," was how Dad put it.

So, when Dad asked whether me and my girlfriend, Paula, would like to accompany him and Mum to the charity dinner and auction that Elwin was organizing, I accepted straight off. It wasn't the sort of thing that the firm had ever done under Brian's direction, and although Dad could see the point as a way of entertaining and impressing clients, he wasn't naturally motivated by such events.

When the evening came, the four of us looked each other up and down and couldn't help but laugh. Mum and Paula kitted our red-carpet celebs, with us men as stiff as skittles in dinner jackets and bow-ties. Although my parents had a nice lifestyle, ostentation wasn't one of them and that'd rubbed off on me. We were more jeans and wellies and picnics in the rain, although we all agreed that just this once we had scrubbed up a treat.

As soon as we arrived, despite the room already being packed, Elwin swooped down on us with the insistence of a vigilant seagull.

"Look at all of you," he shouted. "Fabuloso!" Kissing Mum and Paula, shaking hands vigorously with Dad and me, laughing and talking incessantly, he was the complete antithesis to Dad who just stood there, smiling. Unlike Brian, who although extrovert, had been much lower key, Elwin was like a sixties DJ who'd spent too much time alone. It was difficult to imagine how the two men got on.

Mum, of course, had met Elwin before so I guess she was comparatively immune to him whereas Paula and I were unprepared for the power of his personality. Of course, I was familiar with the expression 'he fills a room' but after meeting Elwin, I now understand the full meaning of that phrase. Although he wasn't physically large, he seemed to suck the impetus out of everyone, leaving them acting as fawning minions. Not that he was unpleasant. Far from it. As Dad said, you could see why he was so good at winning and retaining business. Watching him in action, endlessly circulating, chatting, laughing, complimenting, teasing, pressing the flesh, his impact was irresistible.

And yet, and yet… there was an air of superiority about him. A sense of patronizing supremacy in his manner that even played peek-a-boo when he spoke to Dad. Nothing you could put your finger on, and knowing Dad, who although laid-back was nobody's fool, there would have been trouble if it'd been too obvious.

In the lull following dessert, the MC put out a reminder about the auction prompting those who hadn't settled on their level of commitment to flick anxiously through the catalogue.

"What are you going to bid for?" Mum asked Dad.

"Lord knows. Nothing we want is in there."

"Oh, I don't know. Maybe the wine for a holiday. You'll have to make at least one bid and it must be a good one. You are one of the hosts, after all."

"I don't think that matters. The best tactic is to

bid low for everything, thereby pushing up the amount that someone else pays. Then everyone wins."

"That's a classic accountant's view. Typical you."

"But true!" he laughed.

At that moment, Elwin descended, touching down once again like a predatory bird in a pool full of sprats. "So what have you got your sights on tonight, old bean?" he asked, punching Dad lightly on the arm. "Not likely to be you scooping the biggest bid of the evening, is it? Not with the moths in your pocket."

He laughed, loudly, but quite fondly, at his own summation and we all smiled politely. It was difficult to tell exactly how serious he was, but a glance at Dad showed that this was part of an ongoing commentary, a running joke wearing more than slightly thin.

Dad snickered, nevertheless. "Yes, but the most moths are often found in the deepest pockets, so don't base your economic predictions on unreliable evidence."

"Very Zen, Dad," I said. From a lifetime's experience, I knew, like Mum, that you could push Dad too far, especially when drink was involved, and this was no arena in which to stage the new partners' first falling-out.

Once started, the auction proceeded at a brisk pace. Paula and I decided to bid for a case of wine. Not something we yearned for, but we felt it showed goodwill. We were well outbid. One by one the lots fell. A few went to senior employees, but in the main the successful bidders were clients.

"Nice to see your agency doesn't bill you so much that you can't afford to treat yourselves," the auctioneer, himself a client, quipped at one stage.

Elwin made his presence felt in most of the big-money lots, driving up the bidding with determination. In almost every case, once an eye-watering figure had been reached, he conceded to the other bidder in a way that suggested that they'd both been eyeing up the last cookie on a plate -- *No, you have it. Please, your need is greater than mine.*

A few times he won, whooping with delight, even though he'd paid dearly for something which one suspected, for him, was neither novel nor particularly desirable. However, he was playing the game and playing it well.

Dad, however, was still following his stated strategy. He played around when the bidding was low and then withdrew. From his body language alone, it was obvious that he had no intention of serious participation.

When the last lot came up, Elwin was in line for the highest bid of the evening, twelve thousand, two hundred pounds. The diamond bracelet was presumably intended for his decorative, number three wife.

The final lot on offer was a painting, an abstract which the catalogue described as 'an outstanding study of the human condition by one of this century's most visionary new artists.' The artist's name wasn't familiar to me, and I suspected many others might not have heard of him either. I was intrigued as to whether the merits of the piece would be enough to generate some significant bidding.

The work was large and colorful and not at all the sort of thing my parents liked, so it was no surprise that Dad continued to look uninterested. I'd pretty much lost interest myself until Elwin bid thirteen thousand and it seemed it was all over… until Dad raised his hand.

Mum and I looked at each other.

"Nice one," said Paula softly.

The bidding between the two of them seemed jovial and good-natured to all intents and was made even more so by the auctioneer's sardonic commentary which continued to a breath-taking level.

"Fifteen thousand, seventeen, twenty, twenty-three thousand. Do I hear twenty-four? I have twenty-four. Do I hear twenty-five? Twenty-five? I have twenty-four thousand and nine hundred pounds!"

Elwin shook his head. "Yours," he said to Dad, and grinned. But his smile was forced, weary, and bore every sign of it having been a long night.

"Sold!" the auctioneer said.

Dad looked unruffled, as if it were something he did every day.

Twenty-four thousand, nine hundred pounds? *Explain how that happened, Dad!* We all thought it, but unlike the crowd who surged forward to congratulate him, we remained silent. Even on the way home, no more was said. Undoubtedly Mum was furious, and Dad, well, sometimes with him it's best to keep quiet.

"He did it to show Elwin that he's still top dog," I whispered to Paula later that night as we lay in bed contemplating the evening's events.

"I don't think so. That's too simplistic. I reckon it was an act of support, a public acknowledgment that he accepts Elwin and trusts him. After all, to spend twenty-five grand just like that, he'd have to believe the agency was pretty soon going to earn it back for him."

"Maybe," I said. "But I don't think Dad would have been that subtle, besides, would Elwin have even recognized the gesture?"

"Could you ask your Mum?"

"Mmm." We left the conversation there, and I drifted off into a fitful sleep troubled by thoughts of how much we ever really know one another.

The next morning Mum's response was unequivocal. She shrugged and cast her eyes heavenwards. "God only knows, mid-life crisis probably. "Because I wanted to," is all he's said to me." And with that she left the room, underlining that from her perspective, the episode was closed.

Since then, the incident has assumed the mantle of an elephant in the room. Not that it is in any room. Apparently the painting is still in its packing, stowed in the loft where it's been for the past five years.

A few days ago, when I last spoke to Mum, she said Dad had pointedly left the newspaper on the table next to her breakfast plate. *Record Price Achieved by Turner Prize Finalist,* the headline said. Unsurprisingly, she immediately recognized the artist's name.

"But I haven't said anything about it," she reported. "I wouldn't give him the satisfaction."

So it turns out that the once fairly obscure artist may have been an excellent bet. But to expect Dad, the bean counter, to have known that and to have taken such a risk? Surely not.

Although, once upon a time he had taken a huge risk by investing all he had in setting up the agency, and then, of course, throwing in his lot with Elwin.

Perhaps a leopard never does change its spots?

***

Cows of a Lesser Hue
by Bob Dunlap
CWI Contest Finalist 2016 & Judge's Pick

Whenever I meet someone who lives in a different neck of the woods than I, say a thousand miles or more away, and if we get to talking about farms, I always make it a point to ask, "What colors are the cows where you live?"

Invariably, they act a little odd and mumble, "I dunno. Black or brown. Whaddaya mean, *what color are they?"*

"Well," I say, "I dang near plowed into a whole herd of cows one day on my motorcycle, and when I called the state cops to let 'em know, the cop asked me what color they were."

Usually a little puzzled or even frowning, the person invariably asks, "Explain how that happened."

So, this is how it happened.

Early one beautiful summer morning, I was heading to work, flying along down a country road on my beloved Harley, and upon cresting a hill, saw that the road ahead was, alas, covered with cows. I mean *big* cows with *big* horns, and I slowed down in a hurry, weaving through them while yelling to the nearby House of Booger People, "Hey! Your cows are loose!"

Booger People tend to live on the outskirts of beautiful Albion, Pennsylvania, where meth labs flourish and teeth are an option, and the only conciliatory point to existing there is that when the Zombie Apocalypse transpires, all the simple folk who live there will have little to fear.

I've had deer and turkey cross the same road on previous mornings, and dimly wondered what might next be encountered. Perhaps Godzilla or a Giant Pillsbury Dough-Boy. Weaving safely through the assembled multitude, I got to work and told the guys about it, throwing out a few more than my usual share of F-bombs.

We had a little time to kill before we got rolling, so having the State Police phone number permanently memorized, I gave them a ring. A nice-sounding lady trooper answered, and I cheerfully said, "Howdy! I just came through a whole bunch of cows wandering out on the road on my motorcycle."

Fleetingly, I hoped she wouldn't think the cows were wandering on my Harley. Nobody rides my dear old Hog without first laying down twenty thousand cold, hard ones as collateral, let alone a bunch of delinquent bovines… none of which even possess opposable thumbs. "I just thought I'd let y'all know before somebody smacks into 'em. They didn't wanna move much when I plowed through 'em."

"Just a minute," the lady trooper said. "I need to file a report."

"They're on Griffey Road, right on the north side of Conneaut Crick." This referred to Conneaut Creek, of course, but being a hick from the sticks, I'll never be accused of being an urbanite metrosexual, although, if someone really wants to marry their cow, or even another Cow Boy, I would never pass my judgment, because Uncle Willie was the original Sheep Whisperer, and kept showing up at family reunions with Dollies in lace or Doolies in leather, and surely would have happily married the entire flock if his Mormon-centric tribe would have lightened up enough to allow polygamous bestial matrimony.

After a couple seconds, the lady trooper asked, "How many cows were there?"

Recollecting for a moment, I replied, "I don't know. I rolled through them at 40 miles per hour a little after 7 a.m. and they certainly woke me up in a surrealistic manner of speaking."

I tried to remember… can you murder cows or crows? Do slaughterhouses annihilate cows? If you wipe out a consternation of crows, did you just murder a murder? Is it a cluster-fudge of cows or merely a convocation? A herd sure sounds like what John Wayne and his band of 12-year-old junior cowpokes took down the Chisholm Trail from Texas to Kansas, back in the days when the Duke never had to press "1" for English. So I pondered the question and finally said, "Hmmm, I think there was about a gaggle or so."

The nice cop processed this information, and then dropped the $64,000 question: "What color were they?"

"Well, Ma'am, I'm a bona fide hick. This grasshopper was raised in the big country… cow country. I'm talkin' big cow country, if you want to get all high and technical. I've known cow women, typically large-boned ladies who never learned to dance too well without being all liquored up, and I've also had the pleasure of knowing cow men, including one guy named Bob. That dude could process information at the lightning-like speed of a narcoleptic stoner zombie."

Bob's favorite saying was, "Whaddaya doin' that for, Chuck?"

After Chuck patiently explained why he was doing what he was doing, ol' Bob would wander away scratching his head, only to return in about twenty minutes and again ask, "What're you doing that for,

Chuck?"

This partially explained Chuck's penchant for drinking before noon, but Bob is Chuck's father-in-law, so Chuck started buying stock in Coors Lite soon after getting married.

Nonetheless, cows, in all their glory, have never been strangers to me, and I can unequivocally say that all the four-legged varieties I have ever encountered in this universe have either been brown, black or white, or a happily heterogeneous mixture thereof, with no real off-shades to speak of. Although I have heard whispered rumors of reddish, rust-colored varmints that live across the pond in lands having nice-sounding names like Devonshire and Glousmeisterderry. But rust is basically a sissy shade of brown if you want to get down to brass tacks, therefore, I coyly and craftily answered the lady cop, "They were buff-colored."

"Buff?" the she-cop said, soundly mildly perplexed.

"More of a dun color," I replied, not knowing if these were actual colors, but because I had been hassled by one too many cops back in the wild days of my misspent youth. It was a wee bit of fun to harmlessly mess with the girl in blue with a *back at ya* attitude.

In truth, I do remember reading western novels where the cowboy's faithful horse was either a dun or was dun-colored, or maybe it was the color of the cowboy's chaps, although the biker chaps that biker chicks and nerdy, laughable, wanna-be, pseudo-biker geeks wear are, in fact, 99.5 % black. In fact, the last pair of chaps I bought for my last sweetie were glossy black and fringed to the gills, and came with a warning label that read, *Warning! To be used on a motorcycle only! Not to be worn in a bedroom under any circumstances, nor are they to be worn as a lone adornment in a fireplace-lit basement while shooting pool on a romantic Saturday night, listening to mellow music and sipping el vino.*

Although it is a fact that tags, like lingerie and leather, are all delightful to rip off, like the mattress label that warns the user not to remove it 'Under Penalty of Law,' some warnings are best ignored, Grandpa always said. Grandpa also tried to warn me about the dangers of mixing handcuffs and Smuckers jelly, but as with most things in life, sometimes you just have to forge ahead while cursing the torpedoes.

Along with indiscretion, patience has never been too strong of a virtue for this humanoid, and seeking to finish the 20-question Git-Mo interrogation coming from the lady trooper, I added, "Hey, I've gotta get to work. I just wanted to let you know because I'll be headin' down that same road in a 13-ton bucket truck in about half an hour, and if I should happen to hit one of them moo-cows, I might just fill up my freezer, ya know what I'm sayin'?"

"Yes, sir. We'll check it out," she answered, and with that, our repartee ended.

But in retrospect, my 20-20 hindsight immediately started thinking of what I should have said to her question regarding the color of cows.

"What color were they? Why, they were purple."

No wait! I've never seen a purple cow, and you know how that sad cow tale goes, but although she seemed like a nice enough lady, who was probably packin' both a badge and a gun, I have yet to meet an on-duty cop that enjoys any noticeable sense of humor, elevated or otherwise.

Or I could'a said, "What color were they? Oh, wow, man, they were like, cow-colored, ya know? I mean, like, the 'shrooms hadn't really kicked in yet, but these… cows? Is that what they were? Yeah, cows. Oh wow. They were so friggin' cool, man. It's like they floated around like all the animals in that Pink Floyd video. Ya know? The ones with all the animals? I think it was called Pink Floyd Animals. Remember that album with the floating pigs and a song called *Dogs*? Or the one with the barking dog? And it sounded just like my childhood dog, Charlie, and… whoa man, hey, wait a minute, ain't you, like… a cop? Jeeze, I got the wrong number! Sorry!" [click]

Tsk! What color were they? I still can't get over that. Well, let me see… one was a marvelous shade of mauve, another was mostly taupe, there were a couple in delightful overtones of chartreuse, one had the slightest magenta hues, and three wore lovely hints of fuchsia. Delightful, beautiful creatures!

Because the person answering the phone was female, she would undoubtedly know exactly what colors these names represent, but because I'm a guy, along with every other normal guy in the world, excluding starving artists and interior decorators, I don't know what colors they are, nor will I ever know or even care, to be brutally honest.

I used to lease a little Nissan car having the listed color of teal, but it was actually green. No lie. I also used to teach science, and am familiar with cyanobacteria, the so-called "blue-green algae," the stuff of primordial soup, tough little critters that can live on Antarctic ice sheets, procreate in 400-degree ocean-bottom hydro-thermal vents, and party like micro-rock stars inside highly radioactive nuclear water cooling tanks. As such, I can equate the color cyan with blue/green, and I'm cool with that, but it's ludicrous to believe that teal is anything other than a type of duck, let alone a color of a car, let alone a Nissan, let alone a former import formerly known as Datsun.

Sad to relate, when I rolled down Griffey Road twenty minutes later in my 26,000-pound shopping cart, the cows were safely stashed away, and it was back to eating venison and chicken gizzards for me, although I have since scored a kilo of chicken feet, and am now pondering their many uses.

***

Checking Out
by Stevie Turner
CWI Contest Finalist 2016

He parks the car just before the bridge, and walks briskly past the Samaritans phone box. The never-ending stream of vehicles whiz past as they return home, but he decides it is the end of business as usual. It's time to check out.

He stands on tiptoe and looks over the top of the wall down to the river below, mesmerized by the swirling eddies as his eyes follow the grey water flowing past rocky ridges near the bank on its tumultuous journey toward the North Sea. In his head swim a multitude of images; the laughing faces of his wife and son, Kitten and Honey's pouting lips, and Andy's serene features at a group meeting. As he finds a foothold and heaves himself up the wall, he clings to a faint hope that his new daughter will see a photo of her father every now and then. Does she resemble him?

He stands on top of the wall and looks 60 meters down to a welcome oblivion. The wind threatens to tip him backwards, and he sways to keep himself upright. He is unaware of time or the cars slowing down behind him. When he feels a gentle tap on his ankle, he turns slightly to see a woman about his own age looking up at him and imploring him not to jump. One of her hands reaches up in his direction. He takes in her curly red hair and worried features, the growing number of cars parked on the walkway, and the crowd of people who have gathered behind her. He feels ashamed to be causing so much trouble. His life is a mess of his own doing, and now his chaos is impacting complete strangers. What should he do? He wishes everybody would go away.

He drops to his knees, lowers his forehead down to the bridge's cold parapet, and sobs. The woman with the red hair keeps one hand on his back, and he feels the warmth and comfort of it through his jumper. Somebody brings a flask of hot coffee from their car, and willing hands help him down. He feels buffeted by the wind and from a surge of emotion he would rather have kept hidden. His legs tremble with a kind of aftershock, and he falls to the pavement, spent.

He is irritated by the paramedics' overly cheerful manner as they lift him into a wheelchair and transfer him to a waiting ambulance. They ask him why he was standing on top of the Orwell Bridge, but now his mind is a complete blank. He cannot explain how that happened or even why he was up there in the first place. Out of the window he sees the crowd disperse and the cars move away. He feels as though it happened to somebody else.

The lights in the hospital corridors are too bright after the twilight outside, and he blinks in confusion. He is admitted to a side room, and falls deeply asleep after narrating the whole sorry tale and being given an emergency issue of drugs by the on-call psychiatrist.

The sun streams in through the blinds the next morning, but it takes some time to awaken properly. For a few brief moments, he has no idea where he is, but the medical staff bustling around with half-closed eyes brings the previous day's events rushing back with a heart sinking thud. He lies listlessly under thin blankets, keeping his eyes closed as a kind of protective shield.

He does not see the woman with the curly red

hair until she hovers over him and speaks, informing him that she came to visit as she wanted to know how he was doing. Her tone is pleasant, and he realizes she will probably not leave until she receives a satisfying answer. He focuses on her and shrugs.

Her complexion is pale, and her brown eyes search his face trying to gauge his mood.

Suddenly, he wants to be free of his addiction, and feels ashamed of the way it has taken over his life, his marriage, and virtually his every thought. He unburdens himself to her, and he finds she listens intently in the same non-judgmental way that Andy does. He feels a kind of relief on coming to the end of his story, and sighs when the words cease tumbling. He looks up at the ceiling from his prone position, waiting for her to curse him. She doesn't.

She is back the following day, bringing magazines, fruit, and news from the world that he wanted to escape. He begins to look forward to her visits as he recovers under the watchful eyes of the psychiatric team. She tells him how five years previously she had escaped from a violent husband, and how she now works to counsel women in abusive relationships.

When he realizes he hasn't even asked her name, she laughs, throws back her hair, and says they call her *Alice*. He says he has never hit a woman in his life and never will, but that his wife hates the sight of him.

She nods sympathetically and tells him to take it one day at a time.

He asks if they can meet for coffee when he is discharged.

She looks surprised, but taps his mobile number into her phone. She will let him know when she is free.

He returns home to a cold, unwelcoming house, a divorce petition, and moldy food in the fridge. He has no desire to ever look at pornography again. He needs to find a solicitor to help him gain access to his children, and as he stands amidst the wreckage of his life, forlorn, his phone pings with a message.

I would be delighted to meet you for coffee tomorrow. Alice

***

General Tso's Chicken
by Diane Maciejewski
CWI Contest Finalist 2016

Tessa rolled her head from side to side to ease the tightness in her neck. A quick glance in the car's passenger mirror revealed dark circles beneath her eyes emphasizing her pallid complexion. "When did you get home last night?" she asked her husband as he drove her to the airport. "I was so tired I was in bed by ten."

"It must have been near eleven. You were zonked out."

"Eleven?"

He nodded. "You know how things are at the firm these days. Work late or be the next one on the street looking for a job."

She stared down at her clasped hands, now cold and clammy. Michael was lying. She had been awake when he'd returned home well past midnight. Reluctant to confront him in the moment, she had feigned sleep.

"What?" he said as if she had challenged him. "So I stopped for a drink with the guys."

The sourness of last night's breath attested to more than one drink.

She tried to keep her voice light, making an observation, not a criticism. "You've been doing that a lot lately."

Michael slapped the steering wheel with his palm. "You're traveling around the country with Bruce, doing who knows what, but I can't go out for a drink with the guys?"

She retreated to the inner place she'd created as a young girl to escape her father's anger. Business trips had not been an issue with Michael during the first few years of their relationship. A first marriage for her, a second for him, they had tied the knot in their late forties. Both were devoted to their careers. It hadn't been until last year when Michael's hairline retreated like a defeated army and she met her new co-worker, Bruce, that he'd raised the issue.

Michael zigzagged around taxis and limos until finally pulling up to the terminal's entrance.

As she stroked his upper arm, her sigh filled the car and pushed out the silence. "You know I have no interest in Bruce. You're the only man I love. Please, Michael. It's only for a few more weeks until I move into my new position." She opened the car door. "I want us to spend more time together. When I get back, let's make arrangements for that trip to France we've talked about."

Michael stared straight ahead, hands still on the wheel, as she climbed out of the car.

Three days later, Tessa unlocked the front door of her home and waited for the welcome rush of relief she usually experienced when returning from an out-of-town audit. Instead, her chest tightened as she recalled her conversation with Michael in the car. She walked into the living room and took a step back.

The room was company-ready. Magazines were stacked, and the glass on the coffee table sparkled. In the kitchen, the dishwasher hummed. Two placemats, dishes, and silverware flanked a new candle that decorated the center of the table.

The tightness in her chest eased, and she smiled. Though Michael had been contrite in his phone calls about losing his temper, tidying the house was his signature apology.

A note accompanied the rose on her dinner plate. "Off to White Pearl to pick up General Tso's Chicken. Back by 7:00."

Tessa licked her lips, imagining the garlic and spicy red peppers spreading their blistering heat across her tongue. Michael had introduced her to the dish on their first date, and since then she had linked the piquant Szechuan dish with love.

"Love at first bite. Love at first sight," she thought, remembering how taken she'd been by his deep-set blue eyes and the cleft in his chin. She took a moment to breathe in the flower's fragrance, but was disappointed by its hothouse mediocrity. Still, it was a gesture of affection that Michael rarely made.

Her worries and fatigue dropped away. The clock on the microwave flashed 6:50. She had enough time to take a quick shower and slip into something sexier.

She pulled back the shower curtain and groaned. Would her husband ever learn to clean the hair from the shower drain? She grabbed several tissues and wiped the ceramic tiles. About to throw the wad into the wastebasket, she froze. Strands of long, black hair were sticky with soapy residue. She fingered her short tresses and pictured what was left of Michael's iron-gray hair.

Pain sliced across her forehead like a razor. With the pain came an image of a firm, naked twenty-year-old standing under the shower head, and Michael handing the bimbo her favorite strawberry-scented shampoo. She slumped against the shower stall as her will to live sank. Was Michael having an affair? Adding this evidence to his late nights, what else could she possibly think? Unless his daughter, Cassie, had visited. The teenager could have dyed her bottle-blonde hair black.

The aroma of Chinese take-out accompanied the bang of the kitchen door. "I see your suitcase, Tess. Where are you? Time for dinner."

Tessa pushed herself away from the shower stall. It would take only a moment to clear up the matter and lay her fears to rest. Then she would enjoy the evening with her husband. Clutching the clump of tissue, she walked to the kitchen.

Steam rose from the take-out boxes on the table as Michael opened them. Tessa stood beside him, and he waved the General Tso's Chicken beneath her nose, smiling. Defenseless against the combined aroma of ginger, green onions, and roasted cashews, her mouth watered. She had to swallow twice before she could speak.

"Did Cassie visit while I was away?"

Michael spooned rice onto her plate. "Is that enough?" He added an extra spoonful. "Cassie? Nah, Cassie doesn't have time for her dad."

As if she rode a roller coaster, Tessa's stomach dropped and then rose to her throat like a golf ball. Though she was afraid of raising his ire with questions, she was more frightened of living in a marriage of secrets and lies. Locking her knees to keep them from shaking, she opened the wad of tissue to expose the glob of hair and laid it on the table. She pointed to it as she stared at him. "This came out of the shower. Explain how that happened." Her voice quivered.

Michael's brow creased. "What? The hair?" He shrugged his shoulders. "I guess I forgot to clean the shower."

Fear formed a noose around her throat, but she

refused to be strangled. "Whose hair is this, Michael?" Her voice was soft, but steely. "It's not mine. It's not yours." She paused for a moment to fight back the tears forming in her eyes. "What's her name?"

Michael threw down the spoon. "You think I was with another woman while you were gone? That she showered here? Maybe that's because you've been soaping it up with Brucie!"

She wasn't sure which hurt more… the thought that Michael had been with another woman, or that he believed she had been unfaithful. But what if his accusation was simply a way to deflect his own guilt? Her father had blustered and blamed others when he was at fault. She bit her lip as the tears trickled down her face. How had their marriage gone so wrong?

Michael reached out and wiped her tears from one cheek and then the other. "Aww c'mon, Tess. Don't go dramatic on me. It must be Byron's. He showered here yesterday."

"Byron Meyers, the teenager next door? Why on earth would he shower at our house?"

"One of their pipes sprung a leak yesterday, and they had to cut off the water. Byron came over covered in grime from changing the oil in that jalopy of his, smelling like he'd run a marathon. Said he had a date with his girlfriend and begged to use our shower. I couldn't say no."

Tessa hesitated. She had seen a plumbing truck parked outside her neighbor's house more than once. And Byron did have shoulder length hair, black like his father's. Still… Michael had lied to her before.

"If you don't believe me, ask Byron. He was in his yard shooting hoops when I came in. Go out and ask him."

She took a hesitant step toward the back door

and stopped. Questioning Byron was the same as declaring outright that she didn't trust Michael. She took another step. And another. She had to know for sure.

The thump of a basketball hitting the rim of a metal hoop greeted her as she stepped into her yard. "Hi, Mrs. Wilson," Byron called.

"Hi, uh, did you shower at my house yesterday?"

A blush bloomed across his cheeks. "Yeah, I did. Hope you don't mind. We had a plumbing problem, and I had a date. Sorry if I left a mess in your shower. My mom's always telling me to clean up after myself. Guess I forgot."

Tessa closed her eyes and pressed her hand to her heart.

"You okay, Mrs. Wilson?"

"Yes… yes, I'm fine Byron." She took a deep breath. "How did your date go?"

"Karen said I smelled real good." His ears turned red.

With her head down, Tessa turned toward the house. She had allowed her imagination to team up with her insecurities and ambush her. Michael had told her the truth, and she had doubted him. How must he feel? To make matters worse, he seemed as suspicious about her behavior as she was of his. When had they lost faith in one another? How could she restore what they had lost?

She dragged her feet as she returned to the house, rehearsing her apology under her breath. She had to believe it wasn't too late to make things right. Gathering her courage, she opened the kitchen door quietly.

Michael was on his cell phone, his back to the door. "Can't talk now," he said. "She'll be back any minute. Love you, Ann." He pocketed his phone and turned. The cleft in his chin twitched and sweat broke out above his upper lip.

The fiery tang of General Tso's Chicken peppered his betrayal and scorched Tessa's heart.

***

Falling for Change
by Nellotie Chastain
CWI Contest Finalist 2016

"Amen." Preacher Porter's eyes remained closed. The mad rush to exit the building always troubled him. *Lord, I can only trust you to take the words I've shared and settle it in their hearts*, he thought. His eyes followed Hannah and Joshua as they walked out. Something was troubling them. *Don't know what's happening in their lives, Lord, but be in it for them. Joshua's a good man. He just refuses to believe.*

Hannah glanced at her husband when he reached for her hand. The look on his face was new to her. Wisely, she waited.

A sawmill worker and farmer, Joshua's outside work kept his tall body lean and tanned. His hair was the color of the coal his daddy mined until black lung disease ended his life. Hannah was as blond and beautiful as Joshua was dark and handsome. Their high school sweetheart years stretched into twenty years as husband and wife. Angela, their eldest, was beginning college. Silas, their youngest, was beginning high school.

Hannah and Joshua were quiet toward each other. Since conversation normally came as easy to them as breathing, Hannah's mind raced. What was going on with her husband?

In the middle of the swinging bridge, Joshua stopped. Grasping the supporting cable, he leaned over the edge. Below, the shallow creek was clear and calm. A school of minnows darted back and forth.

"Joshua?"

Turning, he shoved his hands into the pockets of his black jeans. "Don't tell me you really believe all that stuff." His arm swung toward the small, white church building situated above the road.

Searching his mahogany colored eyes, she knew he wasn't just joking. He didn't give her time to answer.

"If Jesus is everything you say He is, why would He even consider jumping off a building just because Satan supposedly tempted him? Explain how that happened."

Hannah reached out to touch his arm.

"Naw," he jerked away. "Can't have it both ways. Either He's real or He's a fake. I don't think I'll be going back to church. At this point, Jesus himself would have to change my mind."

A lone tear slid down her face as she chewed her lower lip. "Honey, I left the chicken cooking. Want to help me with the dumplings?" The heel of one of her white pumps caught between the wooden slats.

Hearing her gasp, Joshua jumped to catch her. The bridge tilted. As he flew over the edge, the last sound Joshua heard was Hannah's scream.

"Walk with me, Joshua." The deep voice sounded as if it could command legions, yet its softness was like soothing honey.

Looking down, Joshua wobbled when he saw schools of minnows fanning back and forth under his feet. A warm surge of peace flowed through his body from a hand that grasped his forearm.

"Come, Joshua."

"But, we're walking on the water."

"It's no big deal. I do it all the time."

Gingerly moving his feet forward, Joshua stole a glance at the barefooted person by his side, who, like himself, was dressed in black jeans and white shirt.

"You have some questions for me?"

"Yes, sir," Joshua said. It was difficult concentrating while his eyes followed the marine life under his feet. "As a matter of fact, I do."

"You'll get used to that soon," Jesus said. "I think your question was, how can I be everything I'm said to be and still be tempted by Satan?"

"Yes, sir." Forgetting the water beneath his feet, he looked eye to eye with Jesus. "I've read your Bible and I go to church almost every Sunday, so I know most of what the Book says. But I just can't make some of that stuff jive with my way of thinking."

"Exactly," Jesus said. "Your way of thinking is your first problem."

"I don't think I've got a problem." Joshua puffed up like a riled dog. "Either you're this great Jesus, or you're not."

"I am."

A large bass in the creek swam under Joshua's feet.

"Every word in that Book is truth. Some of it is difficult for people to understand because they don't have the Holy Spirit to help them."

"I don't know about that. I go to that church up there on the hill. It's not one of those Holy-Roller places." Joshua had never given any thought to Jesus laughing, so when sweet sounds echoed off the clear water and bounced up into the clouds, he smiled... until he looked down.

Jesus' hand rested on Joshua's forearm, calming and steadying him. They now stood at the apex of Joshua's church.

"The roof Satan and I stood on that day was much higher than this, but look around."

Joshua's eyes darted from the roof to the world around them. He forgot the roof and surveyed the panorama that wrapped around them. The creek, tree-covered mountains, homes and children playing.

"Satan thought he could tempt me into making a show for everyone, to prove that I am who I am. Why do you think I didn't prove myself that day, Joshua?"

"If you're really Jesus, you wouldn't have to."

"You're a wise man, Joshua. A little stubborn, but much wiser than you realize."

Joshua's arms flailed like windmill blades. For the third time, Jesus' hand held his arm. Clamping his hand over Jesus', he began to calm. To his amazement, he realized the cable supporting the bridge was not moving, even though he and Jesus were now standing on it.

A peace he had never before experienced infused his entire soul, body and mind. Tears spilled down his cheeks as he looked into Jesus' love-filled eyes. His head nodded. "You are who you say you are."

The light of Heaven shone from Jesus' face as he wrapped Joshua in His healing, forgiving embrace. "I am."

"Thank you, Jesus," Joshua said. "I'll never doubt you again."

"Joshua, please don't leave me." Hannah's tears dripped onto his face. "Help is coming, please hang on." With her legs in the creek, she cradled Joshua's head in her lap. Her shoulder-length hair clung to her face as tears refused to stop.

His eyes blinked.

"Joshua!" Her voice bounced across the water like a skipped rock. "Joshua, can you hear me?" She didn't hear the sound of running feet across the rocks as help arrived.

"Hannah," he whispered. "Kiss me."

"What?"

"Kiss me."

Sobbing, she bent to place a trembling kiss on his smiling lips.

"I'm hurt, but I'll be okay," he murmured against her wet cheek.

"Joshua, how can we help? Where are you hurt?" His brother, Dan, knelt in the creek beside them.

"My head hurts the worst. And my back hurts, but I don't think it's broken. My heart is fine."

"Your heart?" Dan looked at Hannah. "Did he have a heart attack? Is that why he fell?"

Joshua's hand cupped Hannah's face as his eyes looked deeply into hers. "No, Dan, I just got a little too clumsy."

Hannah kept watching his eyes. *He's trying to tell me something.*

"Think you can stand?" Dan asked, careful not to move any part of his brother's body until they were certain more damage would not be done.

"Let's try." Feeling Hannah's hand on his chest, he looked at her. "It's okay, sweetie." She carefully inched her way from under him.

Dan and several friends gathered around Joshua to lift him to his feet.

Hannah's eyes squinted as she watched his face for signs for distress.

His tan face quickly paled when they had him upright. "My heart's fine," he chuckled. Just as he winked at Hannah, his head rolled forward. Blood stained the collar of his white shirt.

Carefully, they carried him to the truck. Dan had tossed a mat into the back before speeding to the creek bank. One hundred and seventy pounds of dead weight took some time to load onto the mat.

Hannah climbed into the truck bed to ride next to Joshua. As the truck jostled up to the gravel road, she noticed a smile on her husband's face. "Joshua?" She placed her mouth next to his face.

"Not to worry, sweetie, my heart's fine."

"Obviously, you're not fine," she said.

"It's just a bump on my head." Joshua reached across his chest and grasped her arm. "Hannah, Jesus changed my mind."

"What?"

"Jesus and I took a walk. He's everything you say He is."

"Joshua," she whispered. Her heart thumped as she realized how close she came to losing the love of her life.

Two stitches closed the gash on Joshua's head. An ice pack reduced the swelling. After a thorough exam, the doctors decided to keep him overnight for observation.

As Hannah drove Joshua home the next morning, they drove past the gravel road that led down to the concrete bridge, and he asked her to pull up to the swinging bridge.

"Why?"

"I just want to stand on it for a few minutes."

"Oh, honey, I don't think so." Her heart began to thump.

"It's okay, sweetie," Joshua said. "I promise."

Slowly pulling to the side of the road, her hands trembled as her fingers folded into his. Sensing her fear, he kissed the top of her head.

Clinging to his hand, Hannah followed him to the center of the swaying bridge.

Joshua found the spot where his body had landed, and his eyes followed the flow of the clear, blue-green water.

"We walked there," he said.

"Where?"

"Jesus and I walked on the water down there."

She remained silent as tears burned her eyes.

"Yes, ma'am. I walked with Jesus right along the top of that creek. Then we stood on top of the church looking out over the community." His hand grasped the bridge's cable. "Sweetie, we even stood right here where we are. Jesus' feet were right here." Tears were now rolling down his cheeks as his hands patted the cable. "He talked to me, and He showed me things." His voice caught. "Hannah, He changed my mind."

Wrapping her arms around his waist, her wet face dampened his shirt.

Slowly, he knelt in front of her. "Hannah, I need to ask your forgiveness for my stubbornness and unbelief."

Laughing through her tears, she said, "The only thing I'm having a hard time forgiving you for is sailing off this bridge."

"That was rude of me," he said. Their laughter was sweet.

After helping him stand, they held hands as they looked at the creek one more time.

"Why did it take Dan so long to get here?" he asked.

"What do you mean?" she asked. "He was here in minutes."

"No, it couldn't have been that quick," Joshua said. "Jesus and I walked way down the creek, and then the church, and…" His voice trailed off.

"From the time you fell and when Dan and the others arrived, it couldn't have been any longer than three minutes."

He slowly shook his head and a look of deep sorrow crossed his face. "Maybe it was all a dream. Maybe it didn't really happen at all."

"How do you feel in here?" Hannah patted his chest.

He covered her hand with his and held it against his chest. What began as a hint of a smile grew wider. He nodded. "He really was here. I walked on the water with Him," he said. "Jesus changed my mind. I certainly fell for that change, didn't I?"

Unseen by Joshua and Hannah as they ambled back to their car, a brilliant form in black jeans and white shirt smiled. With one finger held high, He said, "One more, Father."

Hannah spun around. "Was that thunder?"

"Of course not," Joshua said. "The sun is shining."

**

Old Scruff's Jar
by Cara Minahan
CWI Contest Finalist 2016 & Judge's Pick

The glass jar caught my eye as the shop's light reflected out through the window. The bells on the door jangled as another customer entered Jolly Jim's Stop N' Shop and stood behind me in the long queue. I did not turn, but waited with a pack of corn chips in one hand, tapping one foot. My mind wandered to my wife, Michelle. She and I had been married for eight long, miserable months.

Eight months ago, I ran off the field after beating Dartmouth in a soccer game with heart soaring and fists in the air. I knew something was amiss when I saw Michelle wasn't dressed in her uniform to play in the women's game, and her soft, olive complexion hung in a sunken, pale expression.

Through cheers, whooping and hollering around us, she asked me to follow her under the bleacher stands. It was then she informed me through tear-filled eyes that she was pregnant.

Now, I'm no inventor, but I have a theory about time machines. I believe the human mind makes us go back and forth between past and present, fantasy and reality, more then we want to. So, I revisit that awesome feeling of the Dartmouth victory at least once a day. It occupies my being to the point where all my senses are activated. I can smell the spilled Budweiser on the bleachers, the crowd still cheering and hollering while we stood there in seclusion as Michelle wept in my arms. All I could do was hold her. Halfheartedly.

Then I remember a wave of guilt after everyone had left the stadium. By that time it was dark, and we were still under the stands. Me, in my grass stained uniform and pads, helmet thrown on the ground. She, bawling.

Finally, Michelle dried her eyes and whispered, "This is no way to welcome our baby into the world. I don't have a malignant tumor. I'm carrying our child."

Our child.

The words echoed in my head until all I could hear was white noise. Michelle barely tipped the scales at 100 pounds and I stood over a foot taller and weighed 230, but I swear, in that moment I never felt smaller.

Michelle was nice enough, though I prefer more exotic looking women. I didn't know much about her other than she had the most amazing legs, and she made one of the best goals ever during an overtime match against State College.

I just didn't know the stuff that mattered. What was her favorite movie or her mother's maiden name? When did she want tea? With or without sugar? I never really thought about those things. To tell you the truth, I didn't care. But she *did* like corn chips which was why I was here at this stupid shop. A tap on my shoulder pulled me out of my flashback and daily self-loathing.

A scruffy, older gentleman stood behind me in the line. He gave a deep-throated chuckle. "Thought this was a convenience store, not an *in*convenience store, eh?"

I was not in the mood for any conversation and rolled my eyes rudely.

"Ooh. Whas'da hurry, Bill Murray?"

"What?" I turned and looked at him so coldly

that for a second his grin flickered. "Look, just leave me alone" The corn chips were half crushed under my clenched fist.

"Listen, Chief!" Old Scruff continued. "I calls 'em how I sees em. Yer so ignorant to what's right in front of yuh. You ain't happy and it makes ere'ybody else who comes near yuh feel the same. I can tell. I know. I seen it."

"Sure thing, old man. Whatever. Get lost." I spat out the words and turned away.

"Know what yer problem is? Yer livin' in the past, boy. Too proud to see what's right in front of yer snubby lil' nose." He made a motion toward me, looked me right in the eye, and said, "You ain't happy."

I gave up at this point. I was already late for dinner, stuck in this low class Jolly Jim's Stop N' Shop, and now I was bickering with some hobo. I cracked my neck to the side before replying under my breath. "Yeah, well. My life completely sucks, so..." I trailed off. I had never said that out loud, which felt like I was kicking myself in the rear. Then I noticed his jar. It was so clean it sparkled under the fluorescent lighting, a stark contrast to his frayed and grubby clothing. "Explain how that happened."

His demeanor changed and he stood up straight. "This? Aw, Chief, lemme show ya." He removed one fingerless glove, revealing a scabby, dirty hand, and reached for a small piece of paper lying on the bottom of the glass jar. He unfolded it and placed it in my hand.

The barely legible word scribbled on the back of a store receipt in yellow crayon read, *Happiness.*

He had misunderstood me, and I was irritated. I reached the front of the queue and paid for Michelle's corn chips and waited while the old man paid for a bag of trail mix.

We left the store together.

I handed the piece of paper back to him and squinted at him. "Is this some kind of joke?"

Old Scruff let out an exasperated sigh before opening his trail mix. He shook his head at me. "Listen close now. You may be an ig'nant yuppy, but I know you ain't that dumb. Yer still young." He placed the note gently back into his jar. "You only get one life… just one. It don't always go the way we plan. We jus' need ta love our lives before the good Lord takes us away."

I interrupted Old Scruff, ashamed at being so ignorant and rude to him. We weren't so different, he and I. He was smarter than I, and the guy was undoubtedly homeless.

I pointed at the jar. "I've... I've been looking for that. Happiness. Everywhere. Where do you find it?"

We walked across the parking lot together. A train could be heard in the distance and the sky was a faded orange hue, like God himself came down and painted it so.

"You can spend yer days complainin' and mopin' about them days ya can't get back, or choose to be happy. Chief, I know this to be true. But this... this here is my happiness. You don't jus' find it, see. You make it! I made it myself. It be with me where'er I go, even when I cain't see it."

"Who are you?" I inquired, as serious as stone. I reached for my keys and unlocked my car, placing the half-crushed corn chips in the passenger seat.

Old Scruff turned in my direction and smiled a toothy smile while doing a curtsy. "Me? Why, I be Jolly Jim himself." He waved at me. I knew he wasn't being serious, but I admired his humor. And as quickly as he came, he was gone, whistling *Three O'clock Blues* as he disappeared into the darkness.

I pulled in the drive at our cottage in silence, still bewildered about Old Scruff. I heard the piano, a house warming gift from Michelle's parents, before I opened the front door. Michelle was playing an unmistakable Billy Joel song I once mentioned I loved. I had no idea she even played the piano, and I suddenly felt as small as I did the day she told me she was pregnant.

Michelle turned and smiled at me. Somehow, she looked different. It was almost like I was seeing her for the first time.

She looked beautiful. Was it possible I could be this big of a fool, just now realizing the simple, clear fact, eight months down the road?

She tucked a few strands of curly blonde hair behind her ear. "Hey!" she said in a melodic tone. "I didn't even see you there. I'm sorry about earlier -- hormones. Know what? I made pasta! I, um... know you said you like meat sauce as opposed to marinara, so I got your mom's recipe." She trailed off and continued playing the piano.

I said nothing and stood in the doorway, shifting my weight onto one foot and leaned on the panel. Maybe this would be the wall our child would measure his height on. Every kid has one of those, right? "Hey, Michelle?"

She stopped playing Vienna and gazed up at me with intent. "What's up?"

"I've been thinking lately and…" I scratched my head and laughed to myself a little. "What's your favorite tea? How do you like it?"

Her eyes filled with surprise. "Jasmine!" she

said with a pound of excitement in her tone. "I like it with honey, usually after dinner. And I just ate. Why?"

"Because," I said, still leaning on the panel. "It's important."

Hours passed and the moon shone through the skylight in our bedroom. I closed my laptop for the night and turned toward Michelle. She was sound asleep as she usually was around this hour, with a copy of *Pride and Prejudice* atop her pregnant belly. I removed the book and tore a tiny edge of paper off.

Getting up quietly so I wouldn't wake her, I rummaged through my nightstand for a pen. With a swift motion, I wrote the word just as Old Scruff presented to me hours ago.

Happiness.

I shut down my mental time machine. I didn't want it anymore. I glanced at the word one more time as I sank into my pillow.

Happiness.

And for once, I didn't feel small.

Everything made sense.

***

Antics
by Linda Kay Christensen
CWI Contest Finalist 2016

Growing up on a farm brings back many memories. The long summer days left lengths of time to create those memories.

Our two-story white house faced south, with a lane running alongside to the west. At the end of the drive, a large red barn bordered the east side. Across the back stood a hen house for the laying hens, and a chicken house for the chicks growing up to be Sunday dinner. A corncrib, a small red wood machine shed for extra storage, and the pigs were located nearby, with our cattle residing on the east side of the barn.

My older brother, Dan, was always the creative one. Three years my senior, he led and I followed. One time we raided the garden to make mud pies. Our first violation was the use of a sharp knife and the second was pulling up half of the carrots, cucumbers and beans. Keep in mind it takes a variety of vegetables to make a superbly colorful mud pie composed of water, rich topsoil, and of course the vegetables. We then shaped them into pies to dry in the sun.

Trouble came knocking when Mother found out after putting my two younger siblings down for a nap. Not finding our culinary delights so delightful, she exclaimed with her hands on her hips, "Explain how that happened!" Dan had disappeared and I faced it alone. Guilt set in after the lecture on starving children in China.

Dad often stored a wagon inside the old barn. A

rope used for baling in the hayloft hung across the rafters. With one end attached to a tractor, the other to a hayfork, Dad pulled bales up into the barn loft.

One day, Dan decided it would be fun to swing from this rope playing Tarzan, not realizing the rope had slack in it. Swinging down from the tractor seat toward the wagon, the rope slipped and Dan conked his shinbone into the edge of the wagon. He limped sheepishly to Mother who was working in the garden. Looking up at his very white face with blood running out of his trouser leg, she once again exclaimed, "Explain how that happened!"

Dan took charge of the pigs and I of the chickens. The water faucet we used to fill the drinking containers for the animals stood in one corner of the chicken yard. Dan carried a five-gallon bucket of water to his pigs, while I utilized a small pail to fill the chicken water dispensers.

During another escapade, we simultaneously arrived at the faucet, and while waiting for the buckets to fill, I flicked a small amount of water on him. He cupped his hands, dipped into his bucket, and splattered some back at me. I then grabbed a nearby ladle, filled it with water, and against his protest emptied it on him. Unable to back away fast enough, you guessed it, he emptied his entire five-gallon bucket over my head, drenching every inch of me. Running into the house to dry off, madder than a wet hen, I ran into Mother in the kitchen, who exclaimed once again, "Explain how that happened!"

Imaginative Dan decided to build a tree house. A tree begging for a house stood behind the old hen enclosure at the edge of the barn. At least that's how Dan and I saw it. One exceptionally strong branch extended over our heads, making it easy to create a ladder on the tree. We trudged across the barnyard carrying lengths of board for the project. Nails, a hammer, and a saw from Dad's workshop made a makeshift floor for the house. Both of us pulled it up to the branch with a rope where Dan nailed it into the long branch of the tree.

The first side of the house went together easily, our stockpile reinforced with more trips to the woodpile. I cannot remember how long it took to complete the project other than it was getting dark when we heard Dad calling. Dan was so proud of his project that he beckoned Father to come see the tree. The response was not what either of us expected. Looking at the remaining pieces of wood and the makeshift floor on the tree branch, he said, "Explain how that happened." Dan was crestfallen.

He described the tree house project and the wood and tools. What we didn't know was that the wood had been intended to build a structure on the concrete pad to store ear corn after harvest in the fall. The next day, we pulled out all the nails and disassembled the construction. We were in trouble not only for the use of the wood, but for the danger of falling from the tree. Apparently nails in a tree aren't exactly good for it either.

In early summer, our adventures took us to Little Niagara. On a gravel road running perpendicular to our street, a culvert under the road provided cool water and a small waterfall as it tumbled into the creek. We spent many hours there doing nothing. Loading our bikes with makeshift coffee can buckets, we peddled down the road, stopping to pick strawberries and marvel at who found the largest berry, as these were relatively small but tasty.

Beyond this creek road, our road became a steep

hill called Litwiller Hill. On this gravel road, the challenge was to go down the hill as fast as possible on the bike.

Dan went first.

My bike skidded into loose gravel, the wheel twisted and caught, and I flew like a little bird over the handlebars. I can still see the ground coming toward me as I crashed, with the bike a mangled wreck and the strawberries scattered.

Dan took my strawberries, and I walked my bike back up the hill, crying from the pain of the scrapes on my hands and knees. After reaching the top of the hill, I managed to ride the bicycle back home and walked into the house under the scrutiny of Mother, who exclaimed (you guessed it), "Explain how that happened!"

Iodine and some soothing oil soon covered my gravel burns and scrapes. I remember when Dan and a friend decided to loosen a bunch of screws in the ceiling of the school bus and handed them to the driver when they got off the bus. The bus driver and the school didn't find it humorous. Dan and his friend, Tom, were marched into the principal's office.

"Explain how that happened!" the principal demanded. They recounted how several screws in the bus were loose, so they just removed them. Their sentence included replacing all the screws with a proper screw driver and spending time in the study hall during recess.

Dan and I always had a lot of explaining to do. He was usually in more trouble than me because "he should know better." Each of us had chores, and we helped with the garden, canning, hay baling and other farm projects. After the work, our lazy summer days filled with games of cops and robbers or cowboys and

Indians. We were required to play outside, even to use the outside privy. As we grew up, our explaining had to do more with traffic violations, dents in the cars, getting caught smoking, and running out of gas and such.

Life is an adventure for all of us. Growing up on a farm adds a different dimension for creating fun and entertainment.

***

Ends and Beginnings in Prague
by Stewart Hase
CWI Contest Finalist 2016

I'm not sure what awakened me. All I heard, as the early morning greyness eased though the thinning drapes, was Helena's soft breathing with her arm draped over my chest. She liked to spoon in bed as if making claim, holding on. A desperation and inevitability, as if nothing was permanent. Twenty years my junior, she didn't know it, but we had already parted.

Perhaps it was the taste of stale alcohol and a raging thirst that lifted me to consciousness. Unable to sleep when the mind and body is crying out for recovery, it was often that way. What is sleep for anyway? They say it's the same as death except you wake up. Is it another way of preparing for the inevitable? Life is a series of separations, ending in the big one.

I inwardly groaned at my depressing thoughts and wondered from whence they came. As one grows older, is there a need to be introspective? Where does truth come from?

Rolling over to face the window, I was now awake and my brain on a roll. I needed coffee bad, but it was too hard to get out of the warm sheets. Symbolizing the start of the day, I wasn't ready to face it just yet. Better just let things be still for a while.

Age makes hangovers more difficult to manage. And pretending all was well and ignoring the symptoms of incipient liver failure was no longer an option. Fine when you're twenty-two. It's less acceptable thirty years later.

Slowly, I remembered the night before. We'd gone to a pub in Dlouhá, just off the Old Town Square, even though it meant competing with the tourists who stream into Prague year 'round. It was spring, Italians swarming everywhere, along with a few Brits, and a smattering of Japanese on group tours. They're ever so polite as you step in front of their snapshot of King Wenceslas or the Russian bullet holes in the National Museum.

Spring was late this year and the daytime temperature was around minus two, sometimes with a foray into the positive. All of Europe had experienced a cold snap lasting for weeks. Nature was getting us ready for the ice age, spurred on by climate change.

Helena and I had met up with friends. Drinking plenty of beer and wine, the banter went on until about eleven. We barely heard the band playing Irish music along with a violinist speaking in a Czech accent. Being an Aussie, the language was still a struggle even after several months. I admired the way Europeans were multilingual.

Mind you, I argued, it didn't look too good with the Euro collapsing in a dead faint all over the place. And now Brexit. The problems of the Eurozone eventually proved too much, and the party broke up with a groan.

With Helena and I left to our own devices, I was ready for a main course disagreement.

"It's not just the weather in Prague that is Kafkanesque," I'd said, as the wine took control. A melancholy hung in the air. It's in every step people take. You can see it with their inability to look you in the eye. A lost heroic past, snuffed out during forty years of Russian occupation and degradation manifesting in helplessness.

Helena glared at me over her beer. A wisp of her blond hair had a habit of dropping across her left eye. She flicked the rogue away with her hand.

I could see she was trapped. In endless similar conversations, Helena had made the same point. Change was impossible and nobody cared. Government or organizations sucked the will out of people to live or to try.

It'd been many years since I'd seen anyone get quite as angry about the ruling elite. Not since my union days when passions ran high in the disaffected left. Then I'd been much younger and it was *de rigueur*, as was reading Sartre, Solzhenitsyn, Kierkegaard. It's only in recent years I realized I never understood much of what they were saying. Not sure that I do now, although I have started to revisit them to see if an aged mind has better comprehension. I know now that neither capitalism nor communism makes people happy.

It was then I lit her fuse, and with it, my own realization about me and us. Psychotherapy is all about talking yourself into awareness. And there it was, just as the words spilled out of my mouth. I had my explanation for the conflict I had felt over the past month or so. "It's your generation that will make a difference. We baby boomers will die off and you can take control and change things, create a new culture," I'd said. I wasn't trying to patronize Helena, but probably did anyway.

"Why should we take responsibility for our parent's mistakes?" Helena exploded. She could swear in five languages with exactly the right emphasis. "They, no you, made a mess of it, and now you want us to make it better?"

"No, it's not that," I responded, even though I had indeed meant it.

Helena raised her knowing eyes to the darkened sky. 'Cynicism knows no bounds,' they screamed.

"Your generation is so alive, enthusiastic, and you have the chance to make things the way you want. I mean, look at the students at the university the other night, and the conference. They have so much energy, are so open to knowing, to learning. It's great. The formula is all there."

It was true, well, at least for me. The young are the hope to lift the gloom, shake off the shackles and write a new history. Depression is like a red rag to a bull. Psychologists want to save the world to save themselves. The Mandela Effect, a symbol of lost hope. We can't let it win. It is a foe to be beaten, lest it find its way into the collective consciousness of the human race. Carl Jung in Prague. It makes sense in a weird sort of way. There is nothing altruistic in encouraging the young to patch up our mistakes as a narcissistic manipulation at best.

Helena was in full stride now. "Why wouldn't we want to spend our time on things that are important to us? There are other things to look after in the world rather than the sacred Eurozone. Most of the rest of Europe think we are second-class citizens who belong with the Russians."

"Anywhere east of Berlin is not Europe," I butted in, taking the red herring with both hands.

"It depends on what history book you choose to read. Some would say Russia is part of Europe. All from the same stock probably, although those to the west of Berlin might disagree," she argued. Helena brushed her lock of hair away while throwing her head back. "Let me explain it to you, seeing as you asked," she rebuked. "Forget the Russians. Depression, this 'learned helplessness,' as you keep calling it, comes from forty years of oppression under their regime. And before them it was the Nazis. We are the victim of extremists to the right and the left." Smiling, despite herself, she realized the cleverness of her phrase. Helena looked beautiful, as mixed emotions churned within.

Anything but optimism would be contrary to the spirit of her youth. She and I both had hope. It just got buried under the weight of a generation's experience. We wanted the new republic of Prague to see the past and acknowledge it's hurt from the damage done. To not be chained to it. A new future was coming. There were new shoots on the branches of the trees. Life and the history of earth is a constant cycle of beginnings and ends.

Moving Helena's arm without waking her, I sat up slowly and eased myself out of bed. Gulping a bottle of stale water on the table, I retrieved my clothes strewn about the floor and my socks and shoes amidst the dust under the bed. My small sports bag sat in the corner packed with all my worldly goods aside from the computer case propped up against it.

I admired Helena asleep one last time, then shut the door and left. I do not often look back, but this time was different. Perhaps it was the sense of having an opportunity to do so much more. I think getting older does that to you, though it may be an illusion of wanting to be a part of a future that is no longer yours.

The truth is… my time is gone, and Helena's has just arrived.

***

The Promise
by Phyllis Campbell
Judge's Pick

Spring is a place of magic on Potato Hill. Not quite a hill, and not quite a mountain, it watches over the little settlement of Jennings Gap. One week it's immersed in a dark, silent gloom called winter, and next the frozen earth is alive with the yellows, reds, greens and golds of tiny wild flowers. Lilies, planted by early settlers in long forgotten graves, add brilliant color to the local tapestry.

During the day, the locals love the symphony of bird songs. Nights are quiet except for the voices of hundreds of insects, and the hoarse croak of frogs down by Meadow's Creek. Occasionally, a panther sends its primitive call into the night, just as it did hundreds of years ago.

While spring sang in all its glory, Granny Rose sat in the bentwood rocker that had stood on the front porch since her daddy finished it eighty years ago. Her hair was as white as the snow that cloaked the mountains, and time had stolen two inches from her already short frame.

As she knitted and rocked, she replayed her daddy's stories about fighting in the big war that had set the colonies free from England. She'd been almost ten-years-old at the time, but what did she care about wars? She was busy frolicking with her five younger brothers and sisters, and spying on their older sister and her boyfriend.

Only she remained.

The rest had been taken in less than twenty-four

hours by diphtheria, and only God knew why she'd been left alive, but here she sat on this pretty spring day, fixing to keep a promise.

"Please, Granny Rose, say you'll go," Mrs. Wilson, the preacher's wife pleaded, taking the last sip of her mint tea. "You promised her the day I took her to school that you'd come and hear her sing. That was twelve years ago, and you've never come yet."

"No excuse," Granny said as she looked down at her cup. "I can't do nothin' 'bout when babies need to be born, or little ones havin' the fits and nobody else is way up on the mountain to help but me."

"Well, nobody will need you this year," Mrs. Wilson said. "I've arranged for Dr. Bradford in Pleasant Grove to take any emergencies."

Granny Rose could have reminded her that doctors wanted money, where she took what folks had… a bushel of apples or potatoes, a chicken, or nothing if times were real hard. She knew it wouldn't do any good to mention that, so she just stirred her tea.

"This is a big thing in her life. It's her last recital before she graduates and goes to Massachusetts to teach music. Don't you want to hear her sing?"

"I want it more'n I've ever wanted anything in my life," Granny Rose said, "but I can't. "I'd shame her… an ugly old mountain woman like me. Ms. Wilson, her world ain't the same as mine. Up here on the mountain in this little old cabin, things are different. That's why I gave her up so she could go off to school, and live with you and the Reverend between times. It was like givin' up a part of myself."

"But you introduced her to the world of music," Mrs. Wilson said. "You sang the old folk songs to her, the songs of the mountains. You introduced her to the music of nature, the songs of birds and of the streams.

Please. She loves her Granny Rose."

"All right. I'll be there, and I promise, nothin'll stop me this time."

"Thank you, Granny Rose." The preacher's wife surprised them both by giving the frail woman a hug. "I'll come for you in the buggy a week from today."

When the day came, Granny was as nervous as a bird in a room full of cats. Her dress wasn't very nice – just a fussy looking thing someone from the mission had given her. It was an awful shade of green, and the way it fit, it made her look like a twig walking. Her shawl was right pretty, though. She'd knitted it herself from hand spun yarn using the pay she got for delivering Celie Slaughter's seventh baby.

All them children I delivered, and here I am without a chick nor a child, she thought. They had lost count, her and Ben, of the times they'd hoped and lost. She didn't often let her mind go over such things, but there was something different about this day, and she found herself praying, and not just her usual prayer of thanks either.

"Lord, you know you is the only one who knows this, but I'm tired, and sometimes, Lord, I'm lonesome. I love them pretty flowers, and the birds, and the creek makin' its way out to the river, but Lord I'm ready to be with you and my Ben, and maybe even find them little babies that I never even got to hold here on earth."

The sun went behind a cloud, and her mind wandered back to a night of wind and rain, so hard that it came down sideways. She'd felt unsettled all day for some reason, and when she heard the horse and jingle of harness she started to gather up her things before the knock come at the door.

It was Bob from the big house, way down in the

valley. Bob always looked odd with his big head, and ears that stuck out like the stubby handles on a jug, and his eyes that seemed to look in two directions at once, but what with the wind blowing his black hair every which way, he was right down scary. Granny had learned long ago, though, to take folks as they was, so she opened the door wide and said, "Get in out of the rain, Bob, and tell me who's in trouble."

"It's Mrs. Talbot and Bertie, what takes care of the house. Says she'll die if you don't come. She says to tell you it's her time, and she's been laborin' since this morning."

The last was a pretty good imitation of Bertie Taylor's voice, and Granny Rose couldn't help smiling. "Why ain't they callin' on the doctor like they usually do?" Granny said, picking up the birthing bag she kept ready.

"There's a big tree down 'cross the road just past the cemetery, and Uncle Clem says nobody's gettin' by tonight."

The Talbots came from the North soon after the war between the North and South, and to them, everything and everybody Southern was beneath them, and that most certainly included the likes of Granny Rose.

"I've got a notion not to go," she muttered, but she was putting on her coat.

It was a long hard night, but come dawn, Mrs. Talbot delivered a little girl, a tiny thing with a cry like a kitten. At first Granny Rose thought maybe all was well, until she saw the face, and even she, who had seen some pitiful sights, drew back. Where the eyes should have been, there was nothin' but raw, ugly skin around the little eye sockets.

She managed to shelter it from the mother, but

the father turned pale and motioned Granny Rose to the hall. She tried to hand the baby to Bertie, who turned away, so she carried it with her, wrapped in a warm towel.

Mr. Talbot was a fine looking man, tall with broad shoulders and brown hair, just turning grey at the temples. To granny, though, something cold as Meadow's Creek on a winter day shone in his brown eyes. "For God's sake, woman," he hissed, "take that thing away. It ain't even human!"

"It's your baby, sir." Granny Rose barely managed to add the last word.

"It's a monster, not a baby. Get rid of it. You've done it before, and don't tell me you haven't. Those mountains are full of graves nobody knows about. Take it away, and I don't care how you do it. Just get rid of it."

"I've never done such a thing in my life," her words were dangerously calm, "and I ain't startin' now. This is a breathin' livin' person, and she's got a right to live same as you and me."

"I understand," he said. "How much money do you want?"

If she hadn't been holding the baby, she would've slapped him. Of course, she'd got rid of unwanted babies for girls that didn't have a husband, and women that had ten others, but she'd taken them down the mountain to the mission, and they gave them to people who wanted them. Nobody would want this sad little soul… nobody but Granny Rose. So in the end, she took the bills he offered. This baby, her little baby, would need things she couldn't buy.

"You're goin' to live," she whispered to the baby as Bob drove them home in the old buggy. "Yes, sir! You're gonna live with me and my old goat, Nanny

Girl, and I ain't gonna call you Baby no more. Your name is Hope."

And they'd lived together, the old woman of the mountains and the little blind girl, exploring the trees, and naming the plants Granny Rose used for healing potions, and singing... always singing. Granny Rose had known it wouldn't last, and it didn't. Six years later, Mrs. Wilson came to tell her about a special school.

"She can live at the school during each semester and with us for holidays," Mrs. Wilson said. She'll learn just like children who can see. It's her chance, Granny Rose... her chance to live in the world like everybody else."

It took the light out of her life, but she had let Hope go. And now, eighteen years later, Granny prepared to hear her sing. *I'm comin', Hope. I just need a little rest*, she thought.

Hours later, the preacher's wife said, "I'll tell Hope after the reception."

"Who found her?" the superintendent of the School for the Blind asked.

"I did," Mrs. Wilson said. "She was sitting there in her rocker with the sweetest smile on her face. At first I thought she was asleep." She shook her head sadly.

As the applause came to an end and she left the stage, Hope felt a familiar hand reached for hers. "Granny Rose! You came! You said you would. I love you so much." Hope's face lit with joy as she chattered about the concert. She tapped her white cane against the floor as she wandered away, one hand outstretched as if holding onto a loved one.

The superintendent stared at Mrs. Wilson. "Did you see that?" he said. "Explain how that happened."

He let out a breath and leaned against the wall for support.

Mrs. Wilson dabbed at her eyes as tears slipped down her cheeks. "Granny Rose said nothing would stop her from being here. I guess it didn't."

***

Steps
by Erica Kasper
Judge's Pick

The sleek, gunmetal-gray sports car zipped along the highway, intermittent streetlights throwing orange streaks across the hood. Traffic was light. Few people drove into the city this late on a Sunday. Austin rested his palm on the gear shift as his face twisted into a scowl.

He would still be in his overstuffed chair watching basketball if his wife hadn't called.

If Emily hadn't done what she did.

Emily.

Austin's grip tightened on the steering wheel and he slapped at it. He'd had it with that child. What was she thinking? Sure, the 13-year old struggled with depression, anxiety and teen drama, but how could she do anything *this* stupid?

He'd helped raise his own teenage daughter a decade ago and he recalled her emotional outbursts and irrational rationalizations. He remembered when Dana broke a living room window to get back into the house after sneaking out, and how she had "borrowed" his car before she had her driver's license. Dana had been a bit of a wild child, but Emily was something else.

Emily made her mother cry.

The GPS navigator directed Austin to an exit ramp, and he followed it to the hospital. Ahead, an ambulance pulled into the ER entrance with flashing lights but no siren.

Austin had his choice of parking spots. His

phone chimed, and he glanced at the text message as he got out of the car. It was from his wife, Beth.

Are you close? it said.

He palmed the phone and pushed the tip of his thumb against the keyboard. *I'm walking in.*

After a moment, another text appeared. *Follow the signs to emergency and look for room 12.*

K, he answered.

Austin knew Beth hated the one-letter reply, but he was seething under the skin and didn't care right now.

The double doors of the emergency department loomed ahead, and Austin pushed the *open* button on the wall to activate them. They swung open with a groan.

Austin's hands balled into fists. He hated hospitals. Bad experiences were linked to hospitals. His father had died in a hospital, and his mother had died in one a few years earlier. Her room had filled to overflowing with beeping machines, a rhythmic ventilator and the smell of antiseptic and decay. He remembered saying goodbye to her while a nurse hovered nearby.

And here he was again. He hated everything about it. In this moment, he almost hated Emily.

Austin stepped aside as a pair of EMTs pushed an empty gurney past him.

Two minutes later he spotted Room 12 and stood in the doorway, preparing himself. The light was on, but the curtain drawn, and for a second he thought about turning on his heel and leaving. But Beth needed him. This was the part about *for better or for worse.* He took a deep breath and pushed the curtain aside.

Emily sat upright on a hospital bed. She stared

at him with wide eyes as he walked in.

He barely had a moment to register her before Beth rushed at him.

She stretched out her arms to him, but then seemed to think better of it, settling instead for touching his arm. "Hi," Beth said. "I'm so glad you're here."

He could feel her searching his face. He knew the expression she saw there was blank. Anger made him stoic, and he knew she could feel the tension radiating from him.

Her hand dropped away and she began wringing her fingers together. "She's okay for now," Beth said in a low voice. "They think she threw up most of the pills. They're doing some more blood work."

Austin's vision reddened at the edges, but he forced himself to focus. He studied his wife's face. She had been crying, of course, and the little mascara she had left was smudged and streaked. Her running shorts and t-shirt were comfortable for hanging out at home but not ideal for ambulance rides or hospital rooms. She confirmed his thought when she shivered.

Mostly, she looked tired. The time machine of crisis had worked its merciless efforts on her face, leaving a pale weariness under her eyes.

Austin's jaw tightened. "Why did she do it?"

Beth's shoulders slumped. "I don't know. She doesn't want to talk about it. She says she just wanted to sleep."

The defeat in her voice wrenched at his heart, and he turned his gaze to Emily.

She was motionless on the bed, legs outstretched in front of her. She had wrapped her arms around herself, and she looked small. Her face was ghostly white.

He bit his tongue to avoid saying something he'd regret.

The curtain swept back and a man in scrubs walked in.

Beth greeted him as the doctor, and she introduced Austin.

Austin nodded and stepped back out of the way. *I'm not much good here,* he thought. "I'm sorry, honey. I have to go." He turned to leave.

Beth's hand on his arm stopped him. "The doctor said Emily can eat something. Please stay with her while I get something. Let me have your keys and tell me where the car's parked." Her eyes pleaded her case.

Reluctantly he said, "Sure."

Beth's look was grateful as she grabbed her purse and turned to the girl in the bed. "I'll be right back, okay, sweetie?"

Emily nodded, and Beth and the doctor left the room.

They stared at each other with nothing to say and then looked away. The TV in the upper corner of the room was on the Food Network and they both pretended to watch it.

Austin had the sudden thought that, with Beth out of the room, he could talk to Emily. He could tell her how disappointed he was in her. How much this cry for attention was hurting her mother. He could say the things his wife might not be ready to say.

Tell me what you were thinking was on the tip of his tongue. *Tell me how that many sleeping pills seemed like a good idea. Explain how that happened. Did you really want to scare everyone? Did you really want to break your mother's heart? I thought you were smarter than that. I thought you were better than that.*

He looked up at Emily and found her staring at him again. Her blue eyes looked sad. Profoundly, achingly sad.

His almost-spoken words shriveled on the vine. Instead, he simply asked, "Why?"

Her expression didn't change, but her eyes suddenly grew shiny with tears. She shook her head. "I don't know." Her voice was barely more than a whisper. "I… I don't know."

A wave of warmth spread through Austin, and the anger began to ebb. He looked at his stepdaughter with fresh eyes and read her pain. He saw a kid weighed down with a heart heavier than any child should have to bear. He saw Beth's little girl. *His* little girl.

He eased onto the bed and wrapped his arms around her, pulling her in close. He felt the tension leave her body as she snuggled against him like a small child.

Their eyes met, and then silently they both turned to the TV.

***

The Invisible Rabbit
by Märt Puniste
Judge's Pick

Larry spent most of his hours behind a sheet of paper. Painting meant everything to him, but he could never think of himself as a true artist. He was a poser, a loser unable to accept the lack of greatness in himself. There was no beauty in his work. No striking truth.

He finished a painting of a rabbit, let it fall to the ground and walked on it as he went to bed, thoroughly disgusted. As his eyes closed, he begged the universe to release him from his curse, but, as was true every night, no help came.

The next morning, a blasting knock on the door woke him and he tossed on a t-shirt used for mopping paint. Nausea and a busting headache almost put him down, but the knocking continued and he staggered to answer it. His agent stood at the door.

"Hey," Billy said. His fingers tapped against his thighs. "How are you?"

"Okay," Larry lied, finding it hard to maintain eye contact.

Billy stepped inside the apartment and cleared his throat. "I'm sorry, but I can't represent you anymore."

Larry knew it was his own fault. When was the last time he gave Billy something decent to sell? "I understand," he said with a shrug.

Billy toed the piles of paintings on the floor. Noticing the picture with the rabbit, he stopped.

For a full half-minute, he stood like a statue. Finally, he pointed to the bunny.

Larry grabbed the thing from the floor and

studied it. "What?" he said.

Billy, who couldn't seem to form words, nodded and pulled the paper from Larry's fingers. He left the apartment.

Hungover, Larry walked to a bar close by. It was also the most depressing place he knew, but the darkness hid Larry and it felt like home.

He spotted Amy right away. She was sitting at her usual spot under a burned-out lamp. She was beyond suicidal. With her, it wasn't a question of *if*, but *when*. Larry took a seat next to her and ordered a whiskey.

The bartender gave him a nod and turned to find the cheap stuff. Without a word, he gave it to Larry and turned away.

"He doesn't act right," Larry said.

"He found out he's dying," Amy took a sip of her drink and went on writing in her notebook. There was no concern in her voice.

Larry knew why. She considered the man lucky.

When Amy took another drink, her sleeve slipped down her arm exposing scars. They were thick stripes, the way a person cuts when they're serious.

Larry raised his eyes to hers and she just said, "Yeah. I tried but didn't get the job done. Spent a week in the nut house."

Larry gave her a nod and took a sip of the whiskey. It didn't burn any more. "Have you heard from Christian?" he said. Their friend had stolen from both of them.

Amy stopped writing and met his eyes. "He's off the wagon, shooting up somewhere, I think."

Larry sighed and finished his drink. He felt sorry for Christian, the same way he felt sorry for himself and Amy, but what could he do? "Well, I guess we won't be seeing him anytime soon."

Amy sighed and returned to her notebook.

"What are you writing?"

"Eh, just putting on the finishing touches," she said.

"To what?"

Amy closed the notebook and signaled Bob for another drink.

"You know, I've always said I have nothing to say. When I die, that's it."

Larry nodded and asked for another drink as well.

"When they drove me to the hospital and I was fading in and out of consciousness, it kind of felt wrong. Like, I thought I owed some people some parting words."

"A suicide note?"

"Yeah, something like that." Amy changed the subject. "How's your painting?"

Larry rolled his eyes and finished his second glass. "I think I got fired."

"You *think?*"

"Billy came by, and pretty much told me that, but then he took off with one of my paintings. A terrible one at that. I have no clue what he's doing with it."

"You think all your paintings are terrible."

"They are. Have you finished the book you're writing?"

Amy shook her head. "Can't. I realized there's no decent ending to that story." She paused, setting her line of thought in order, "Maybe, sometimes, to end a story, you need to end the person writing it."

They stayed silent for a while.

Amy reopened her notebook and Larry looked around the bar.

It wasn't noon yet, but the regulars were there.

The old man at the bar who ordered one drink after another until he couldn't stand. Beside the window, another old man, known for his gray suit and hat, always drank alone. No smiling faces at this bar.

Larry's phone chirped with a message from Billy. "See you at your place in five. Great news!"

"What's going on?" Amy asked.

"Don't know, but got to go."

"Okay."

Neither said goodbye, and Larry walked back to his apartment.

Billy's face glowed. His smile stretched from ear to ear, and his eyes shone like diamonds. He grabbed Larry in a bear hug. "Larry, my boy." He'd never done that before.

"What's going on?" Larry said as he pulled away.

"I need to show you something," Billy said. He pulled out his phone and showed it to Larry. On it was a picture of the rabbit painting. "It's something special Larry. Yes, something very special. I don't know how to say it, but it changed me."

"Okay, if you say so." Larry pushed the phone away. Something was clearly wrong with Billy.

"I'm not the only one to think so." Billy scrolled down and lifted the phone again. "Look at that… right there. Read the number of views."

Larry squinted. "Seventeen million? That can't be right. What does that mean?"

Billy grinned. "Wait." He refreshed the page and held it up for Larry to see again. "Now read it."

"Twenty-two million views? How is that possible?"

"You've painted something very special. Take good care of it, okay?" Billy said as he handed the picture to him. "I'm goin' to see my kids. They finally agreed to meet with me. I'll talk to ya later. Yes, sir. That's a mighty fine picture."

Larry looked at the bunny once more. It was so stupid. Why in the world would millions want to see it? He rolled the picture up and headed for the bar to ask Amy.

Christian was waiting for him in the hallway. He looked unwell, but he was smiling. "Larry, my friend." He moved closer, arms stretched for a hug, but Larry backed away.

"I'm sorry for everything, Larry. Can you ever forgive me?"

"Sure." Larry's forehead wrinkled as he studied Christian's strange behavior.

"Man, I was on such a terrible path. So terrible. But then," his eyes opened wide, "I saw your painting and everything changed. Everything, Larry… everything."

"What in the heck are you talking about?"

"The bunny, Larry, the bunny. It took my pain away."

"Christian, are you drunk? Are you high?"

"No, man. I'm great!"

Larry looked at him with a wary eye. "Explain how that happened."

"I don't know. I plain don't know, but I have to go."

"Whoa," Larry said. "Where are you off to in such a hurry?

"You'll think I'm nuts. I'm going to the police to confess a few things. I just feel like this is the time to make things right."

Too confused to deal with Christian, Larry headed back to the bar.

There were crowds on the street. A parade of

happiness. People were singing and laughing.

Larry stared and forced his way through the utopia, happy to arrive at the only place of sanity - the bar of depression.

The man in gray suit and hat was surrounded by laughing friends, and the gent who was known for drinking 'til he dropped was sipping water, lapping through an old photo album with a smile on his face.

Amy was laughing and chatting with someone Larry had never seen before. "Larry! It's so great to see you." She hugged him.

"What's going on?" he said.

"Oh, pardon me, this is Tom. We just met a couple of minutes ago. Tom, this is my good friend, Larry."

"What in the heck is going on here?" Larry said.

"It's wonderful! That painting, the one of the rabbit, I saw it and it healed me. *You* healed me, Larry." She put a hand over her heart and smiled. "No more pain."

Larry backed away, but stopped when he saw Amy's notebook in the trashcan. He pulled it out. "You threw this away?"

"Oh, that thing isn't me. Nothing in there makes any sense. But listen, I'm making dinner tonight. Please say you'll come."

He picked up the notebook and hurried back to his apartment. A new kind of ache pierced him. The Amy he knew was gone. And everybody was happy? He looked at the painting again, straining to see what others had, but to him it was a massive study of idiocy. He ripped it apart. Why was he the only person who couldn't be happy? For the first time, he was truly alone. Tears starting rolling. He sat on his bed and leafed through Amy's notebook.

Dear Larry,

We both know there is no greater pain than living. And what makes it worse is feeling it will never end. I'm suffering in ways even you couldn't understand.

In spite of what we say or the sham of how we act toward one another, I love you, and I know you love me. When you read this, you'll know I finally did it.

Please know there was no other way. Nothing in the world can fix the pain inside me.

What we've had has been so special and those memories are the only thing I'll take with me.

Love, Amy

Larry sat stone-still, crying unashamedly. Amy was gone. Somehow he had fixed her with the bunny picture and in doing so, had lost her forever. He turned the page and saw one more line.

Remember: Maybe, sometimes, to end a story, you need to end the person writing it.

***

One Night in Brasstown
by Victor G. Espinosa
Judge's Pick

Officer Walter Applegate savored his midnight snack, a short stack of pancakes at the local Waffle House, when his radio buzzed with the first call of the night. Brasstown was small and docile, and Walter thrived on quiet nights when he didn't get a single call. Tonight wasn't one of those nights.

His watch read 12:14 a.m.

"Go ahead, Dispatch," Walter said, swallowing a mouthful of food.

A woman's heavy southern drawl spoke in the garbled tone of a walkie-talkie. "Patrol Twelve, I've got an emergency call from a young lady out past the propane station." There was a pause, and then she continued, "This is a strange one, Patrol Twelve, but I think it'll be fun."

Walter sighed as he waved the waitress over for a to-go box. He thumbed the button on his radio. "Diane," he asked, "is that you?"

"Mh-hhhm," she replied.

"Why do you always send these uncanny calls to me? Why not Paul or Greg?"

"Paul and Greg are both busy, Twelve," Dispatch responded. "Come on, you like spice in your life, and we both know you could use more of that."

Walter cleared his throat. "You know me too well, Dispatch." He stood, left plenty of cash on the table, and carried the Styrofoam container to his car.

The voice on the other side of the radio continued. "Nonsense, Twelve. This is strictly a professional relationship between us."

Walter wasn't sure what he'd call their relationship, but 'professional' certainly wasn't it. However, Diane was right. He did need some pepper in his life. Ever since retiring from the Army, life had grown too stagnant. Back in the patrol car, he said, "Ten-four, Dispatch. Send me the address and I'm on my way."

Six minutes later, Walter pulled into the gravel driveway of 190 Dreskin Road. Before him was an aged cabin with a country feel to it and a wraparound porch. Motion sensors lit up the yard and surrounding woods, revealing a sign above the door that read, *Lady Bug Cabin.*

The patrol car's roof lights strobed the night, turning the surrounding area into a rave of reds and blues.

Walter kept his high beams on.

A woman stood on the cabin's front steps, frantically waving one arm for help. In her other arm, she clutched a quacking mallard duck. She was in her late twenties and not unattractive, wearing a simple t-shirt and jeans combo under a heavy black robe.

Walter closed his eyes for a moment and pinched the bridge of his nose. Diane meant for this to be funny, not frustrating, he told himself. Opening his eyes, the woman was still in his high beams, still waving and still holding her duck. He reflected on Diane's odd sense of humor as he opened his door and stepped onto the gravel driveway.

Walter wore his officer's persona… an open mind, heightened senses, and tense reflexes which made him ready for anything. His gaze never stopped scrutinizing the woman's movements for anything that might be hostile as she ran toward him. Nothing stood out.

"Thank God you're here," the woman panted. "I didn't think they'd believe me. You've got to help!"

Walter held out his hands to calm the woman, but she continued hysterically.

"I'm so relieved you actually came," she said through sobs. "You got here quick enough that she might still be in the woods out back. You have to do something before she goes into your town!"

"Who are you talking about, ma'am?" Walter inquired. Speaking over her frightened voice was nearly impossible. "Why don't you…"

"I know, I know," she wailed. "I'm not supposed to call the regular police, but I knew you'd get here quicker than the Ministry and I thought you'd be able to help somehow. You know, maybe do something… to help." The woman broke down sobbing which turned her words into unintelligible sounds.

Walter watched the duck struggle in the woman's arms until she gathered herself together.

"Ma-maybe you can at least warn the town – get everyone out of there. Sabrina hates your kind more than anything. She'd torture you all to death if she could."

Walter took a deep breath before speaking. "Ma'am, I have no idea what you're talking about. I need for you to quiet down and give me the facts about what's happened. Okay? I can't help you if you can't help me, alright?"

"Right," the woman breathed. She visibly composed herself while stroking her duck.

"Now," Walter asked, whipping out his notebook, "tell me what happened from the beginning. May I have your name?"

"They didn't even give you my name?" the woman squealed. "Didn't the person on the phone tell you anything? I spoke with her for ten minutes."

Walter sensed the woman on the verge of losing control again, but for a different reason. He put just the right amount of force into his voice and said, "Ma'am." He lifted an eyebrow at her.

Glaring, she complied. "My name is Rebecca." She indicated the duck with somber movements. "This is… James. He didn't used to look like this, but Sabrina challenged him to a duel and turned him into a duck."

The duck fidgeted in Rebecca's arms and let out a resounding quack.

"Excuse me?" Walter said. He stared at both the woman and the duck, confused. The only thought occupying his mind was how Diane would pay for this.

"You probably think I'm crazy, don't you?" Rebecca asked.

"Ma'am, you just told me someone changed your boyfriend into a duck."

"He's not my boyfriend. He's my husband!" Rebecca shouted, flashing her ring finger. "And that really is what happened."

"Uh-huh," Walter said, rubbing his eyes. "Explain how that happened… if you don't mind."

"Explain it?" Rebecca cried. "I can't explain it. I signed a contract. I'm not allowed to explain it."

"You can't explain it?"

Rebecca leaned in close and whispered. "Alright listen, before the Ministry gets here. Sabrina's a wizard, like me and James. She used a transfiguration spell on my husband even though it's forbidden in a duel." She glanced at the duck in her arms. "And she turned James into this."

Walter's mind worked at top speed but he simply couldn't process her story. It sounded like she lived inside a video game world. He looked at his watch, longing for the solitude of his patrol car and his pancakes.

"I can prove it," Rebecca blurted out. "I know you don't believe me, so let me show you."

"How?" he asked.

Rebecca stood and hoisted the duck higher on her hip, like a mother adjusting a baby's weight. "I can take you to where they dueled."

Walter pulled a flashlight from his belt and motioned to Rebecca. "Lead the way." He knew the sooner he proved her a fraud, the sooner he could report to dispatch and finish his food.

Rebecca walked to the back of the house, a few feet away from the surrounding woods. Ordinary items populated the backyard – firewood, kayaks, lounge chairs. It looked okay, except for a small area. On the grass, next to a line of ferns marking the forest's boundary, lay a pile of clothes, ripped and smoking.

"There," Rebecca said, pointing. "That's where James stood for the duel. He got hit by her spell, fell, and crawled there. After a bolt of light, the next thing I knew, a duck ran quacking around my yard."

Walter knelt to examine the pile of clothes that looked similar to Rebecca's – a simple t-shirt, jeans, sneakers, and a large black robe. Wherever Walter poked the material, fresh smoke and a hideous stench escaped into the night air.

The woman shifted anxiously while watching Walter work, then informed him, "Sabrina left his clothes, but took his wand and ran into the woods."

Walter glanced at the thick, dark forest behind the house, then back to the heap. This wasn't enough proof. It could've easily been planned by some of the town's more mischievous residents who had too much time on their hands. He'd heard of the faux incidents, scandals, and pranks, plaguing the small town in years past with scandalous gossip destroying the reputation of innocent people. He wouldn't let a silly prank get to him.

He stood and walked toward his cruiser.

Rebecca trotted alongside. "Where are you going?" she asked. "Aren't you going to check the rest of the backyard or the forest?"

"No," Walter replied.

Rebecca abruptly halted. "What? Why?"

"Because I don't believe you," he said. "Because I'd like to be ready in case someone with a real emergency needs me." He turned and jabbed a finger at her. "Because whatever chemical you ate, snorted, or smoked has made you believe something so strongly I doubt anyone could ever reverse it."

"You think I'm drugged?" Rebecca screamed. "That's why you won't help me?" Her voice weighed heavy with desperation.

Walter walked to his car and opened the door, addressing Rebecca before climbing in. "Consider yourself lucky I don't write you a fine for wasting my time." He got in, shut the door, and reached for his radio.

Rebecca ranted obscenities and stomped her feet while holding her duck. "You're all so useless. I knew I should've waited for the Ministry with those pointy hats to get here." She glanced at Walter's car and stomped her feet again while yelling, "Useless!"

Meanwhile, the duck sat oblivious in her arms,

quacking occasionally.

Walter hit the radio's button. "Dispatch?"

Diane's familiar voice rose from the speakers. "Did ya'll play nice?"

"You need to learn what a junkie sounds like," Walter said. "Quit listening to their drug trips and quit sending an officer to investigate."

Rebecca suddenly stopped her outburst and stood motionless, as if she'd seen a ghost. She slowly lifted her hand in self-defense.

"Junkie?" Diane asked. "She didn't sound like she was tripping to me. Scared, yes, poor girl, but not high."

Outside, Rebecca mumbled and shook her head violently.

"She was tripping alright. Still is," Walter said into his radio. "High as a kite. Her husband is a duck and now she's surrendering to who knows what."

Rebecca's words grew in volume until they penetrated Walter's car. "No, no, no!" she screamed again and again.

Walter watched Rebecca back away from something only she could see, until a searing flash lit up the night. He shielded his eyes from the burning glare. It lasted only a few seconds, but left him temporarily blinded. He rubbed his eyes until his vision returned, not believing what he saw. Blinking a few times, the image remained.

In front of the headlights was a fresh pile of smoking clothes and two terrified mallard ducks.

He picked up the radio from his lap with trembling hands. "Dispatch, I – I n-need to call you b-back."

**

~*~

If you enjoyed ***Explain! A themed anthology 2016***, please consider leaving a review on Amazon.

If you would like to offer feedback, please email **jay@SouthernStarPublications.com.**

Thank you for reading this anthology.

~*~

Short story contest entries were judged on originality, creativity, style and technique.

A great story can score well in the first two categories but lose marks if grammar, punctuation and spelling are incorrect and if paragraphs are poorly formatted.

Learn how to write professionally at Creative Writing Institute, where every student receives a private tutor. It could be the difference between a top placement, being a finalist, or missing a top spot.

With permission, the contest stories have been edited for this publication while trying to maintain the intent of the original entry.

You can find our previous anthologies on Amazon -

> ***Bargain: A themed anthology 2015***
> ***Wrong: A themed anthology 2014***
> ***Overruled: A themed anthology 2013***

Creative Writing Institute

Creative Writing Institute is an online writing school that provides a variety of writing courses and a private tutor. Our classes are open year round, which means you can begin your course right now. If you need financial assistance, we offer a no interest payment plan.

As a 501(c)3 nonprofit charity, CWI sponsors cancer patients in free writing courses. In addition, we have constructed our courses so visually impaired students can use adaptive devices to enlarge or convert text into electronically synthesized speech.

Our goal: to evaluate you quickly and personally escort you to your highest potential. We will encourage your heart and sharpen your mind.

Our pledge:

- We will tailor your class to meet your needs, aptitude and desires.
- You will have a private tutor who will provide quick and professional assistance all the way through your course.
- You will never be a number to us. Your tutor will interact with you all the way through your course.

Please… believe in yourself. Invest in yourself. If you will make writing a priority, we will do everything within our power to make your writing dreams come true. Start climbing that ladder to the stars today!

Courses:
- Punctuation Review

- Creative Writing 101
- Dynamic Non-fiction
- Short Story Safari
- Writing for Children
- Writing for the Middle Grades
- Writing for the Young Adult
- Fantasy in Flight
- Horror House
- Fundamentals of Poetry
- Flash Fiction
- Novel Writing Made Easy
- Advanced Wordsmithing - coming soon
- Famous Women Poets - coming soon
- Writing Programs for the Blind

Payment plans available at no interest.
http://www.CreativeWritingInstitute.com/

Meet the Team

Creative Writing Institute is the place where people come together from all over the world. We pool knowledge and resources, and God makes miracles happen.

Some folks support this ministry financially, and our hearty thanks go out to them. We also have volunteers who selflessly contribute time and talents. They come from all walks of life – ordinary homebodies, retired folks, and high school/college students. Most volunteers have full time jobs elsewhere, and yet they make time to help others. Our highest praise and thanks go to you.

If you read our **"About Us" page**, you will learn the story of the *Mystery Lady,* a cancer survivor who changed lives with writing therapy. Founder Deborah Owen was so impressed with the lady's story that Creative Writing Institute carries her mantle of personal tutoring and writing therapy to every student.

Our volunteer works come from America, Canada, New Zealand, Africa, India, England, South Korea, Australia, and Italy. If you would like to be a part of this work, either as a volunteer or donor, contact our CEO, **DeborahOwen@CWinst.com**.

Staff Members: thank you to staff members: Mrs. S. Joan Popek, Mr. L. Edward Carroll, Mrs. Emily-Jane Hills Orford, Mrs. Kim Cawley, and Mrs. Diane Robinson.

Contest Judges: thank you to the five judges who gave both time and energy to select winners of the short story contest. You did a wonderful job, as usual. The head judge was Jo Popek, and the coordinator was Jianna Higgins. Supporting judges were Diane Robinson, Emily-Jane Hills Orford and L. Edward Carroll.

Volunteer Staff: without you, we could not possibly keep up with the newsletter, library, blog posting, article writing, editing, posting social media, etc. We salute you, William Battis (age 91!), Julie Canfield, Jianna Higgins, Nicky Hirst, Christine Cassello, Karen Johnson, Kevin Keeney, Erinn Sanders, Michelle Malsbury, and Andrea Cronrod. Please accept our profuse thanks and appreciation!

Donor: this page would not be complete without special thanks to Mr. Albert Dinger for his prayer and regular financial support. God bless.

Special Memorial: our poetry tutor, Mr. Joe Massingham, passed away this summer. We miss him and convey our condolences to his family. We are very grateful for the courses he developed, and they will stand as a memorial to him.

Jay Hirst, publisher of Southern Star Publications: Thank you, Jay, for your many kindnesses and the hundreds of hours you dedicate to CWI. We appreciate your eye for details, accuracy in proofreading, punctuality, and talent in layouts. Our anthology can be compared with anyone's and not come up lacking, all because of your painstaking efforts and leadership. Thank you so much.

Folks, when you need a publisher, check out: **www.SouthernStarPublications.com**

And lastly, we would like to thank those who have passed through our door and left their footprints on our heart. We treasure your contribution and our time with you.

Wishing you the very best ~ Deborah Owen, CEO.